THE
DREAMER
IN THE
UNHAUNTED
HOUSE

IBRAHIM ANDERSON

The Dreamer in the Unhaunted House

peacepearlsusa@gmail.com

Cover Design by Adam Hay
Book Interior Design by Charlyn Samson
Copy Editor Skye Loyd

Identifiers:
ISBN 979-8-9854359-1-7 (paperback)
ISBN 979-8-9854359-2-4 (hardcover)
ISBN 979-8-9854359-0-0 (ebook)
ISBN 979-8-9854359-3-1 (audiobook)

N.I.M.C.I.T

Novels Inspired by Muslim Culture and Islamic Theology

This is a work of fiction. Time and space have been rearranged to depict an entertaining narrative and enjoin moral lessons. Any resemblance to actual persons, entities, or events is coincidental—with the only exceptions being God Almighty and His beloved Prophet Muhammad (or when actual verses of the Qur'an are quoted). The opinions expressed are those of the characters and should not be confused with the author's. Furthermore, NO JINN were solicited or involved, in any way or at any time, during the creation of this fictional narrative.

To Jean,
Whose friendship rescued me
when I was alone in a world
where no one would hear my story.
I am immensely grateful for your loving kindness
and the lessons your love has taught me.
Thank you from the very bottom of my heart.

CHAPTER ONE

The home was built for all seven of Sulaiman's children, even though Nejimah—his daughter—was an only child. It was a home with as rich a tale as could be told, and as sweet a voice as one might ever have encountered. Yet, to hear this sweet voice—to understand the voice of any house—is an effort in futility without the willingness to listen carefully to its story. That is emphatically the case when the house has been a true home. Houses like this have the uncanny ability to tell a tale, and by the unenlightened soul, they are often mistaken as haunted. The question thus arises, what is a haunted house, anyway?

To identify a house as haunted, one must first know the edifice prior to its enchanting. Who lived there? And what lives were impacted when the home was once filled with love? Perhaps there *are* haunted houses … ones that exist in places that have never known love. However, there have *never* been homes haunted like this one—where love was palpable and pervasive in every cranny and nook and every square foot.

This was a home among the houses of the *unhaunted*. They are everything contrary to what you thought you knew about ghosts and ghouls; and they present themselves only to the esoteric—an unusual and gifted few human beings who have gained access to phenomena beyond the five human senses.

7707 Sprite Meadow Court was the home of Sulaiman Sanders. It stood at the vertex of an angle created by the intersection of perpendicular streets that closed one another off. When exiting the residence, the view to the right, along Sprite Meadow, presented eight beautifully designed homes— four on either side of the street—beginning with 7701 to the right and 7702 to the left. Alternately, the view straight ahead encompassed a dozen homes that aligned along Meadowlark Lane. These began with the home of the neighbors to the immediate left. Sulaiman's home, and the semi-private streets that joined in front of it, were comfortably nestled in the heart of a suburban subdivision known as The Meadows. It was a family-oriented neighborhood—luxurious and serene without feeling clinical and lifeless.

Today, a magnificent rainbow hovered above The Meadows after a light thunder shower. There was an atmosphere of nature breathing a sigh of relief—consuming the freshness that a gentle pour had left for it to quench its thirst. It was Saturday. Sulaiman had spent his morning preparing notes for his lecture in class that day. He gazed one last time out of his bedroom window, admiring nature's illustration of the rainbow over his backyard. Then he began a final inspection of the particulars inside his home, spraying lavender-scented Febreeze along the way—first the upstairs, then down. Finally, he collected his Quran and the supplemental materials needed for class before heading off to the *masjid*.

Backing out of the driveway, he noticed the same silver Mercedes that he'd seen the previous two weekends parked out front. The driver, Brittany, looked up from her mobile device and offered a smile and wave, followed by a thumbs-up. She expected today's walk-through to be a fruitful one. As Sulaiman drove away, Brittany exited her vehicle to replenish the flyers under the Coldwell Banker Realty sign—which bore her portrait above the tagline "2028 Realtor of the Year."

The prospective buyers arrived moments later, and five smiling faces dashed out of the SUV filled with excitement. This was the second viewing for the parents, who expected their children to love the home as much as they did. This might be their forever home, but they wanted another look before finalizing the decision. Being the ultimate salesperson, Brittany had brought treats for the children—yet another layer of the special touch that garnered her such high praise in the industry. She was certain Sulaiman would receive an offer by the end of the day.

As the realtor unlocked the door to the beautiful two-story home, the children entered first. They were enamored. The home was a spacious 3200 square feet, sitting on a 15,000 square foot lot—most of which comprised a stunning backyard. The front door opened into the foyer, and the first thing one noticed upon entering was the cascading stairwell that wrapped up to the second level. A ten-foot by ten-foot mural of an adorable garden hung in a niche along the stairwell, adding a special touch to the entry way. In the foyer, just above the front door, hung a clever chandelier— too fancy to go unnoticed but not overly gaudy.

Cherry-walnut hardwood flooring lined the entry way and wrapped into the living room off to the right. To the left, a set of double doors opened to an inviting formal dining area, filled with natural lighting. However, Sulaiman had used this room as his den for the past few years. The beautifully updated kitchen could be accessed from either the den or the living room and also invited a ton of natural lighting. A bay window in the informal dining area peered out into the incredible backyard.

Isabella, the oldest of the Romero children, was compelled to take a detour at this point. She opened the door leading from the kitchen into the backyard. She was convinced there was nothing more she needed to see. Plopping down on the patio furniture, she put in her air pods and began to imagine life in her new home. There was more than enough room to install the in-ground swimming pool she so desperately wanted.

While Isabella remained in her outdoor retreat, the rest of the family continued on the tour. They viewed the garage, laundry, and half-bath before returning to the foyer and heading upstairs. There were four spacious bedrooms on the second level, the first of which was an enormous master suite immediately to the left at the top of the staircase. With an en suite master bath, a walk-in closet, and all the bells and whistles, this room checked every box for Mrs. Romero. For Mr. Romero, the necessary boxes were checked by the beaming smile on his wife's face.

The boys, Anthony and Mateo, spotted the game room, which separated the master suite from the other three bedrooms. They ran off ahead of the tour, leaving Brittany and their parents in the master suite. As the tour continued, Mrs. Romero texted Isabella to rejoin the group and come see her bedroom. Eventually, the family made their way into the backyard, where they recapped the tour and discussed making an offer.

A sudden beep from Anthony's smartwatch notified him that he left his TechBot Mini in the house somewhere. His mother would be furious if he left it behind. Thankfully, she had programmed it to his watch—specifically for instances like this. The boys rushed upstairs to find it but again got distracted by the game room. They eventually split up, forcing themselves to resume their search.

Minutes later, Anthony called out for Mateo to come and find him. By now, the savvy younger brother had learned all of his elder's tricks. He methodically scoured each of the bedrooms, making sure to check under beds and in the closets. Finally, he walked into the very last room, where Anthony was certain to be. He peeked under the bed and found nothing. The closet was the only stone left unturned. Mateo opened the door and out jumped Anthony, attempting to scare him. Mateo's heart dropped to the floor and he darted out of the bedroom, screaming at the top of his lungs. He stormed through the kitchen door and into the backyard, raising a ruckus. Through panicked breathing, Mateo explained that his brother had tried to scare him in a game of hide and seek. But his fear had nothing to do with Anthony. Rather, it was the "monster" in the closet with him.

Frustrated with her sons, Mrs. Romero left Mateo with his father and went after Anthony, intent on disciplining him. When she got to the bedroom, however, she found her son curled in the fetal position in the corner of the room, weeping and refusing to open his eyes. She called for her husband, who gathered their eight-year-old son, and as he carried him down the stairs, the rest of the family headed out to their vehicle. No one understood exactly what had happened. However, this would not be the day that the home on Sprite Meadow severed its ties with the life of the man who built it.

CHAPTER TWO

The New Muslims class was held every other Saturday on the second floor in the main building at Masjid Salam—one of the many facilities owned and governed by the Islamic Society of North Eagleton. Sulaiman had taught the class since the day he had been invited as a guest speaker, nearly a decade earlier. He had never missed a class since. For him, it was a blessing more than a responsibility, and those who attended were as beloved to him as family.

There was never a large turnout—usually between six and ten attendees—but the discussions were rich and authentic. A core objective was to provide an open platform for discussing topics that resonated with real-world experience for new converts. Sulaiman's recurring challenge to the class was to understand Islam as an applied lifestyle. "We have to make adjustments in our perspectives," he urged. "Let's take Islam out of our imagination, and place it in our hearts and in our lives. The Prophet Muhammad taught this religion as a practical way of life … not a fairy tale." The class was designed to help new Muslims navigate the inevitable challenges that come with choosing to be a Muslim in America. It presented real-life strategies for real-world problems; but the class was not exclusive to Muslims. No one was ever barred from attending or from asking questions.

Sulaiman sat in the classroom looking over his notes for several minutes. Ten minutes passed and no one showed. That was unusual. Occasionally, there was an odd week when only two or three showed up; but it was extremely rare that no one showed. He strolled to the window peering out into the parking lot. None of the cars looked familiar. Another glance at the clock indicated that ten more minutes had passed. At this point, with no one to teach, he decided to go downstairs and pray *Dhuhr*. Perhaps someone would arrive in the interim.

After prayer, Sulaiman proceeded to return to the classroom; on the way, he met a visitor coming down the stairs. She was looking for the class and inquired whether she had come to the right place. He introduced himself and confirmed that she had. Since no one else showed for class, they decided to sit at a picnic table outside in front of the masjid. Sulaiman was happy to answer any questions she had, and he spent the next two hours doing so.

The young visitor was conscientious but not timid. Her name was Celine. She wore a lilac Foxcroft blouse with long sleeves and a tail that draped below her hips. A decorative scarf covered her neckline and was chosen for the dual purpose of covering her hair, in case she was asked. A light jacket was draped over her left forearm, and in her right hand was a spiral writing pad with an ink pen tucked into the coils. Immediately, Sulaiman could tell that she had done her homework.

Their conversation was polite and respectful but not superficial. Celine had tough questions and Sulaiman welcomed them all. He was committed to ensure that she left with a more thorough understanding of Islam than she came with. His manner was kinder and more respectful than she anticipated; during the conversation, his gentle, patient demeanor was on full display. A welcoming personality made him easy to talk to—which in turn made her more inclined to listen to him. What she found most impressive, however, was an enthralling conviction of faith. This was a man who clearly believed every single word he shared. She couldn't remember ever meeting someone more genuine or whole-hearted in their faith.

As the discourse came to a close, the question in the back of Sulaiman's mind finally made its way to the surface. "Celine, can I ask how long you've been researching Islam?"

"On and off for about two years. But pretty steady for the last six months. Why?"

"As I sat listening to you, I remembered having some of the same questions in my own journey to Islam; and it brought me back to a familiar place."

"Oh yeah? And what place is that?"

"A crossroads."

"Really? That's interesting."

"You strike me as someone very organized—who carefully deliberates over every decision. I think that's admirable … but what's your end goal?"

"What do you mean?"

"I mean, when every answer is obtained, and every contingency is considered, and every 'i' is dotted and every 't' is crossed … what will you do with the information? What do you hope to achieve as a result of your study?"

"I don't know. To learn, I suppose."

"To learn … maybe. To live … more probably. I believe we're all personally driven toward a call within ourselves to live our best lives. I think you hear that call, more clearly with each passing day. But then, there are the questions. Valid questions. Genuine questions. And then there's the crossroads—a place where we indulge in the preoccupation of questions in order to avoid the answers. Honestly, Celine, the answers to the questions you've asked me aren't meant to be incorporated into your knowledge base, they're meant to be incorporated into your life."

"And how do you suppose I do that—become a Muslim?"

"That's not a question for me to answer. Only you can know that. But my advice is to stop thinking and start feeling. What do you see when you look back over your day? Was today a regular day for you, or have you noticed subtle nuances that seem unusual? I ask because, in my view, the timing of your visit is highly peculiar. Today is the first time ever that no one showed for class. I don't think that's a coincidence. I think that's the Lord letting you know that He sees you … specifically you. He knows you have questions and He's ready to guide you to the answers that are specifically tailored to your life. So much so, that He cleared an entire classroom to let you know that you have His undivided attention. So when are you going to trust Him?"

It was a message with a resounding ring to it: stop overanalyzing and allow yourself to feel what's right for your life. Sulaiman was correct. Celine had heard the call and she knew it. But she was afraid. Converting to Islam was an intimidating prospect. Of all the questions she had gathered over the past two years, she questioned her own intuition the most. Somehow though, in this moment, Celine had never experienced greater clarity. So she allowed herself to feel and trusted her own instincts. Since the very beginning, her heart had inclined toward Islam, and today she followed it. "I bear witness there's no god except Allah," she declared, "and that Muhammad is His servant and messenger." With the help of the kind gentlemen she met at the masjid, she embraced Islam.

The sun peeked out from behind the clouds and shone on the unassuming picnic table sitting on the lawn of the Islamic center. Sulaiman grinned as he reached for his phone and remarked that the heavens were smiling because of Celine. She felt that way too. Scrolling through the contacts in his phone, he shared a few recommendations to help simplify Celine's faith journey. Then he passed along the information of two Muslim sisters who would be happy to help her with anything she might need in acclimating within the Islamic community.

As he walked away from the table, a rush of endorphins flooded Sulaiman's central nervous system. The voice in his head celebrated with him, as his heart hummed the sweetest of melodies. He was happy for Celine and even happier being blessed as a part of her faith story. In Sulaiman's view, there was no greater reward on earth than being gifted with moments like these that allowed him to make a contribution to Islam. His faith was singular in its influence over his behavior, and Islam was his fountain of fulfillment.

He had a relationship with the Creator of heaven and earth that couldn't be described as anything but the truest form of love—pure worship. He was an ordinary man by all outward appearances, though his relationship with Allah was anything but. Sulaiman was blessed with the gift of dreams— extraordinary dreams. When he closed his eyes at night, other worlds unfolded within his subconscious, revealing wonders of unimaginable grandeur.

The dreams were exceedingly vivid—filled with color, depth, and images that were indistinguishable from reality. Sulaiman could also perceive sound, and he participated in full conversations that he remembered after waking. Incredibly, he could see himself in his own dreams—traveling through space and time, or lying peacefully asleep in bed. Occasionally, he'd have a dream so astounding that he never wanted it to end; when it did, he tried going back to sleep to find it again.

One such dream occurred during the month of Ramadan. It was the dream he adored more than any other, and every year he longed to see it again, though it never returned. On the seventh night of the holy month, as his body rested in bed, Sulaiman's subconscious stood in an enormous tent, waiting. Others waited alongside him, but he couldn't see their faces. He only saw the face of the one who mattered: the beloved Prophet Muhammad. It was an experience so full of emotion that tears poured from his dreaming eyes, and when he awakened, they continued to pour.

The seventh of Ramadan held a special place in the dreamer's heart, as it was the night he was favored with one of Allah's greatest gifts. Ironically, it was one of the many gifts he received that accompanied the number seven in some way. The date of Sulaiman's birth was September 7, 1977. Besides the sevens marking the day and year of his birth, the name of the month, *September*, carries the same number in its meaning. It was uncanny how the number coincided with significant events in Sulaiman's life: his address, the date he embraced Islam, the date of his marriage, and many others. Even his precious Nejimah—whom he loved more than

13

anyone on earth—entered his life on July 7, 2007. Her birth was announced by a little girl in one of Sulaiman's dreams. That little girl would have been Nejimah's older sister, but she hadn't survived the pregnancy. Sulaiman and his wife, Shifaa, suffered through six miscarriages. Nejimah was the result of their seventh pregnancy.

The children in Sulaiman's dreams were numerous, but two of the dreams were distinct from the others. Twice, he dreamed of his own children before they died in the womb. Each child spoke at great length, imparting wisdom and encouraging their father to remain steadfast in faith. The first conversation occurred during the initial pregnancy. Sulaiman dreamed of a son named Adam who was small enough to fit in the palm of his hand. The tiny tot advised his father with the eloquence of a scholar in the highest order. Sulaiman listened intently, and before the dream ended, he kissed his son, expressing his love and gratitude.

The next day, a scream came down from the bedroom and echoed in the foyer. Sulaiman nearly tripped as he raced up the steps to check on Shifaa. He arrived to find his tearful wife sitting on the edge of the bathtub, pointing in the direction of the toilet. As he peered over the lip of the toilet seat, he found Adam lying on the cold porcelain just above the water line. By the decree of Allah, the tiny human had slipped from his mother's womb. The baby had a peach-opal flesh tone, and the tissue on his back was jagged—indicating that he had been attached to the uterus from an area near his spinal cord. He had tiny black dots for eyes, and he was even smaller in real life than in the dream. He was the size of Sulaiman's pinky finger. Even so, he had already developed ten fingers, ten toes, and a host of other attributes that his parents would never forget.

Sulaiman dreamed of the second conversation when Shifaa was pregnant for the sixth time. It was a girl this time, and her name was Porsha. He thought it peculiar because that was not a name he would normally have chosen, and his dreams usually aligned with his conscious preferences. Still, he listened as the loquacious toddler expounded upon one exhortation after another. She was a most impressive little girl—as intelligent as she was beautiful. She made all the bubbly hand gestures of a happy two-year-old as she conversed using the vernacular of a university professor. It was a wonderful conversation that gave Sulaiman a sense of peace and tranquility. Porsha's final word of encouragement to her father was, "Rejoice in the blessings of Allah and be delighted to know that my sister is coming. In her love, you will find great joy."

Sulaiman would later come to believe that he was mistaken in hearing the name Porsha. Perhaps she'd said "Bushra," because she was the one who gave him the "glad tidings" that the daughter coming after her would live a full and prosperous life.

CHAPTER THREE

Sulaiman's iPhone vibrated in the passenger seat as he pulled into the gas station on the way home from the masjid, though he never noticed it. He was distracted by the emotional high of Celine's great news. A second call set the phone abuzz as he stood oblivious outside the car—daydreaming with his fingers clutching the gas pump lever. The smell of spilled gas reminded him of his childhood, pumping gas for his mother as a young boy. Back then, you could smell the fumes coming directly from the pump. Sulaiman loved that smell—that and the smell of his cousin's fingernail polish remover. He carefully avoided the gasoline-soaked pavement as he replaced the pump and returned to the driver's seat of his vehicle. As he sat down, the final buzz of a third consecutive missed call finally caught his attention.

Reaching across the armrest, Sulaiman grabbed the phone and reviewed calls from Nejimah and both real estate agents. His daughter left an endearing voicemail, telling him how much she loved and missed him. She was recently married and adjusting to daily life away from her dad. She and her husband, Bilal, lived a short drive away, and she checked in with her father regularly—mainly because she knew that he missed her twice as much as she missed him. Hearing her voice made Sulaiman smile.

The other voicemail was from Brittany, about the house. Although she was the buyer's realtor, Sulaiman trusted her more than his own agent because they had previously worked together. He could hear the concern in her voice as she explained what occurred during the walk-through with the Romeros. This was the second incident in as many months, and it was nearly identical to the first. Both prospective buyers were Brittany's clients; in both cases, she had been certain of an offer before the family was frightened away. After listening to the message, Sulaiman didn't bother calling her back. Undeniably, there was something going on here. Maybe it was simply Allah's plan for him not to sell the house right now; but he also considered the possibility that evil jinn might have entered his home.

He pulled into the driveway and said a short *dua* before entering the house. Everything was exactly as he'd left it—with no sign of anything out of the ordinary. This was the same dwelling where Nejimah had lived her entire life, and there had never been incidents like the ones Brittany described until now. Their home had always been covered in the mercy of Allah. Now, all of a sudden, something was disturbing its peace. Sulaiman planned to spend the night in prayer, which was his answer for every problem. He was a man who would ask Allah for anything, and oftentimes—with patience—he got exactly what he asked for. If there were *satans* looking for a fight, Sulaiman was calling the Lord into the battle against them.

He prepared a quick bite for dinner and sat at the table. Nostalgia washed over him as he stared at the empty place setting where his beloved Shifaa once sat across from him. The house felt so big and empty without her. The plane crash that took her life took his heart along with her, and the lingering guilt had left him irrevocably heartbroken. Sulaiman longed for the past, when his world revolved around the two women in his life whose names said it all. Nejimah was his star and the twinkle in his eye; her mother, Shifaa, was the healing for every ailment in his heart. She was his best friend and the love of his life ... and now she was gone. It had been a few years already, but the wound was still fresh and he still missed her almost every day.

The thought of remarrying occurred to him, but he struggled with the concept, philosophically and emotionally. How do you approach marriage when you're certain that you've already loved the love of your life, and what are you supposed to look for when the best-case scenario is second-best? In the end, it didn't seem fair to a potential bride that he was already in love with another woman—even if she was gone forever. So he focused on raising his daughter and poured his heart into his faith and the Islamic community. After five years, he was learning to forgive himself, and he found comfort in knowing that Allah's forgiveness is without limitation. Sulaiman's faith was stronger than ever, and the FOR SALE sign out front was an announcement that he was finally ready to move forward in discovering the next chapter of his life. He finished his dinner and prepared for worship.

A burgundy Quran embellished with gold lettering rested in Sulaiman's lap. He sat cross-legged on a prayer rug, with his hands raised in supplication. An intense night of worship lay ahead of him, which he began by reciting the 286 verses of Surat Al-Baqarah. In this particular chapter of the Quran, there is special protection against evil forces.

Sulaiman called upon the Lord with a sincere heart, beseeching the Creator of all things to protect his home from the evil within creation. Sweat poured from his brow as the intensity within his soul extended beyond its physical shell. His heart rate climbed as he imagined an Almighty Sovereign wielding justice in one hand and compassionate forgiveness in the other. This was the mental state in which Sulaiman found himself as he prayed—at the intersection between paralyzing fear and sheer ecstasy.

There was nothing in Sulaiman's life equivalent to the nights he spent in prayer and supplication. He loved Allah, and he could feel the love of his Master shining down in return. It was an exchange that even angels enjoyed watching. Some nights, they lined in rows to get a view of Sulaiman's prayers going up. Tonight, they numbered in the thousands, intent on catching a glimpse of the exchange between the servant and his Lord. They squeezed side by side—one atop the other—forming an enormous tower into the heavens. They were intrigued by the sight of his heart reaching for Allah's Love and Mercy. Sulaiman's sincerity moved them, and the angels often said prayers on his behalf, asking Allah to grant him special favors.

The astute servant of Allah was aware of the fact that he was never alone—he knew that angels are always present. What he didn't know, however, was the fact that he had recently attracted the attention of another individual—one who was equally intrigued at the sight of his worship. She hid in the closet, where she had frightened the Romero children, waiting for an opportunity to see him again.

The calming rhythm of Sulaiman's recitation wandered through the hallway and into the far bedroom where she waited, notifying her that it was safe to come out. She followed the sound of his voice, as she moved down the hall in a smooth glide, like dust particles. Slowly, she entered the bedroom and stood beside him, mesmerized at the sight of a human who was unlike any other she had ever seen. He piqued her curiosity like nothing before. She examined him, studying everything about him.

Not a single feature of his existence eluded her. She counted the hairs on his arms and every lash in his eyelids, though she was careful not to encroach upon the boundaries

21

of his worship. She never moved in front of him, and she was particularly respectful when he bowed in prostration. Everything about him compelled her attention, but nothing more than the sight of the heart beating inside of him. She was completely captivated by it.

There was a place in Sulaiman's heart where it fused with his soul, and the sincerity of his faith beautified it beyond description. It was extraordinarily spectacular; she had never seen anything like it on earth. He was the reason she tried to delay the selling of his home. Something about this man drew her to him, and she didn't know what to make of it. She needed more time to figure that out.

Sulaiman fell asleep atop his prayer rug on the floor, and he immediately began to dream. He dreamed of a woman—a mysterious woman—who sneaked into his bedroom to watch him sleep. In the dream he saw himself lying on the floor, exactly as he was in reality. The woman floated into his room like a spirit and hovered above his sleeping body, as he lay face-up on the floor. She moved closer until her nose was almost touching his, examining his every breath. Then she hovered above his chest cavity, where his extraordinary heart was encased. She turned her head to the side, sinking her face below the surface of his skin, and placed her ear directly onto his heart. She remained there for several minutes until the heartbeat was usurped by a murmur she couldn't decipher. Eventually, his heartbeat returned and the dream ended.

Sulaiman jumped from the floor after suddenly awakening, only to realize that there was no one there. She was only a dream, albeit an incredibly real one. He gathered himself and began his morning routine in preparation for work. The day came and went as uneventfully as usual, and as he relaxed in bed that night, he thought of her. Moments later, he found himself in the exact same dream, only this time he was in bed. Again, the mysterious woman came floating into his room and proceeded in the same manner as the night before.

Another day came and went, and for the third straight night, Sulaiman watched from the corner of his dream as the incessant female entered his room and placed her ear on his heart. This time, however, she was able to decipher the murmur that interrupted his heartbeat. She heard it perfectly. It started very light and gradually increased in volume. Her eyes widened when she recognized the familiar sound. Sulaiman's heart was speaking, and she knew exactly what it was saying. Then all of a sudden, everything stopped. She was accosted by an overwhelming voice outside of Sulaiman's body.

"Who are you and why do you come here every night? What do you want?"

She was extremely nervous as she looked around, wondering where the voice was coming from. It was Sulaiman's subconscious, surveilling his dream with total anonymity. For the past three nights, she had intruded into his home. He was now past the point of pleasantries; he wanted answers.

Again, he squawked an interrogatory that frightened her to the point she nearly fell to the floor. She quickly collected herself and tried floating away but was immediately halted. Her wrist was chained by the authority of his subconscious. This interrogation was not optional.

"Who are you … and why do you keep doing this to me?"

After recognizing the sound of his voice, her nerves began to calm. She politely responded with an apology: "I'm so sorry for the intrusion. I sincerely meant no harm. I honestly didn't think you were even aware of my presence. I was only curious … that's all. Can I go now?"

There was no answer to her question … only dead silence, though she was yet unable to free herself. Nervously, she waited for an answer, wondering what would happen next. After a long wait, she petitioned, "Excuse me, are you there? Is everything OK? How are you speaking to me when I can see that you're asleep? Helloooo … are you there? Can I go now?"

A faint echo of the voice in the background continuously began to repeat, *"Who are you and why are you here?"* Then she felt her arm release and bolted from the premises as fast as she could. As she hurtled beyond the subdivision, something inside told her to go back. She had a feeling. Perhaps against her better judgment, she decided to return. Racing through The Meadows and into the home, she arrived at the bedroom door—just in time to find Sulaiman waking from his sleep. She didn't dare enter the bedroom, but as she stood at the threshold, she could see his lips mouthing the words "Who are you and why are you here?" He mumbled the words as he tossed and turned one last time before his eyes popped open and he sat up in bed.

It was a monumental discovery for her to learn that everything that happened was only a dream to him. He had no idea—now that he was awake—that she was standing outside his bedroom door. It was an astounding revelation that she struggled to understand. Somehow he was able to accurately perceive her reality inside his dreams—so much so that he was actually able to restrain her. But how could that be? There was only one individual who might know the answer to that question; the time had come for a visit back home.

CHAPTER FOUR

ncle Hakeem was the most righteous individual she knew, and though he never looked down on anyone, his presence could be intimidating. As she made her way through the woods, she felt a bit nervous. She hadn't been home in awhile, and he was certain to give her grief about it. Standing beside the massive tree trunk, she was rehearsing what to say when Aunt Sakina startled her, approaching from behind. Returning from errands—collecting duckweed and daffodils—Sakina grabbed her niece by the hand and reassured her with a loving smile. "It's OK, sweetie," she said. "Your uncle Hakeem barks, but he doesn't bite. Besides, he loves you more than anything in this world."

A deep voice bellowed from within the foliage, "Who's there?"

"It's me. I just got back," Sakina responded.

"And who's with you?"

The loving aunt silently gestured, encouraging her niece to speak up. She finally did. "It's me ... Sky. I came to check in and see how you guys are doing."

With that, an 850-year-old *jinni* emerged from the greenery and looked her in the eyes saying, "Sky? I don't know a Sky. What sort of name is that? I know someone named Samaa." His sarcasm wasn't intended to be mean, but he had raised his niece to be proud of her heritage, and there was always a lesson in the way he treated her. "Sweetheart," he admonished, "Don't let them take your name from you. It may seem harmless, but it starts with your name ... and it will end with your soul." Then he hugged his niece and welcomed her home.

Samaa's uncle was the most respected of all the Muslim jinn in the community. He was born and raised in Islam, and his lineage made him a celebrity—practically royalty. Hakeem's grandfather was one of the jinn whom Allah had mentioned in the Quran when He revealed in Surat Al-Jinn:

Say, O Prophet, It has been revealed to me that a group of jinn listened to the Quran, and told their fellow jinn, "Indeed, we have heard a wondrous recitation. It leads to Right Guidance so we believed in it, and we will never worship anyone as a partner with our Lord."

Everyone always asked Hakeem about his grandfather and the jinn who embraced Islam in the presence of the beloved Prophet. He sometimes indulged the questions but usually found an inoffensive way to refocus the conversation.

He didn't like for Muslims to lavish undue praise on created things, because no one is qualified to take the credit for how they're created. Moreover, he detested the social disease of ranking Allah's creatures based on lineage or other attributes they had no hand in deciding for themselves. He insisted, "Allah is the Creator, and He alone has the authority to judge His creation."

Samaa got settled in and was happy to be home again. She didn't realize how much she missed it. She could tell her uncle had been missing her too. He was playful and talkative as usual, but even when he was hard on her, she could feel his love. He had always been there for her, and he was the only father figure she'd ever known. He was patient and a wonderful listener. Even when she didn't know what to say, or how to say it, she could always talk to him, and that's why she was home. The man in the house on Sprite Meadow Court had turned her world upside down, and she could hardly think of anything else. She needed to talk but didn't know how to approach the topic. She finally decided to jump right in:

"Uncle Hakeem, have you ever heard of a jinni married to a human?"

"What? What on earth makes you ask that?"

"Nothing, really. I just wondered. You always know the most obscure facts. So I figured if anyone knew of something weird like that, it would be you."

"No, I can't say that I have. I'm sure it's probably happened at some point in history, but not to my knowledge."

"I was just thinking the other day about humans and jinn. We go about our lives in the exact same world. We are in every place together, and yet there's a veil between us that forbids them from seeing us and prohibits our interaction. I don't understand that—especially since the evil ones among us have no problem communicating with the evildoers among them. If our ancestor can be mentioned in the Holy Book of Allah in a positive way, why aren't there more examples of positive interactions between righteous jinn and humans?

"Samaa, where is all this coming from?"

"Nowhere. I'm just asking. Look, I know I'm not a good believer. But YOU are, and I don't understand why someone like you can't have a pleasant relationship with another creation who loves Allah as much as you do."

"Listen, you've known me your whole life, and if you know anything, then you know that I'm happy with Allah. I don't have any qualms with the restrictions placed on my existence by my Creator. He is qualified to make that decision, and I'm happy with His choice." He paused. "What's going on?"

"Nothing."

"You know that I pray for my brothers and sisters among the children of Adam, regularly, and I love them as I love all the Muslims. But if Allah didn't create me to be able to communicate with them, well then, I accept that. Now, as for you not being a good Muslim, I think you're as good a Muslim as you will allow yourself to be. I have known, since you were a baby, that Allah made you special. But it's up to you to come back to Islam. When you do, your destiny is greatness. I'm sure of it. Now ... can we talk about what you really came to talk about?"

When she was put on the spot, Samaa completely drew a blank. She opened her mouth, but no words would come out. Everything she had rehearsed was forgotten, and she was left with a complicated situation she had no idea how to explain. Hakeem waited patiently, as he could see her wrestling with the ideas inside her head. He knew Samaa, probably better than she knew herself, and he understood that whatever was on her mind would eventually find its way out. After a long pause that seemed to last an eternity, she solemnly began to explain: "Six weeks ago, I saw a man and I followed him home. I realized he was Muslim when I saw him praying. So I watched him. I could see his heart beating inside of him, and when I did, I couldn't look away. I've never seen anything like it. To be honest, I don't pay attention to the sons of Adam, so it never occurred to me that one heart isn't the same as another. I know they're different, but I just figured it was like a thumb or a nose—basically the same thing in a different body. But this man's heart ... I can't even explain it. Anyway, I followed him again the next day ... and the day after that. A couple of weeks later, I was sleeping in the closet of an empty bedroom in his home."

"*AstaghfirAllah*. This is a transgression."

"I know … it was wrong. But I didn't do anything. I was just watching him."

"OK. So what happened?"

"Uncle, please … I'm trying to tell you. Anyway, I hid in the closet most of time, and I only came out when I heard him praying or moving about the house. Allah is my witness, I never entered his bathroom once, and I never looked at him unless he was properly covered. The thing is, I couldn't leave. There's just something about him. As I waited to get a closer look at his heart, I saw the way he lives, and he reminds me of you. I see in him a man who is the best of his kind, and that makes me want to be the best of what Allah has created in me. Then, a few nights ago, I approached him as he slept and I put my ear on his heart to listen to it."

"Samaa! What were you—"

"But then, something incredible happened. He caught me. He could actually see me, and he even grabbed me. He held my wrist and I couldn't get away."

"*La hawla wa la quwwata illah billah.*"

Hakeem was flabbergasted. They continued back and forth, discussing the details of what happened as he reprimanded his niece's lack of judgement. One thing was clear, however. It was time for her to stop procrastinating with Islam and get her faith on track. When he asked what she heard in Sulaiman's heart murmur, she replied, "The kalimah. It kept repeating '*La ilaaha ill-Allah.*'"

As for the man whose home she invaded, Hakeem wondered about him. How was he able to restrain her—or even see her? Magic and sorcery were out of the question if he was truly a Muslim. So who was he? Would Hakeem recognize him from the masjid, or was he new to the city of Eagleton? A human being capable of interacting with jinn would be the topic of every discussion, yet this was the first Hakeem had heard of him. If this man's dreams gave him an opening into the world of the unseen, that was an extraordinary gift from Allah. The elder jinni wondered what all of this meant for his niece and her future. He forbade her from ever returning to that home and wouldn't hear any backtalk on the matter. Inside, Samaa vehemently objected to the decision, but she had never openly disobeyed her uncle. So she acquiesced.

Like humans, jinn are created with the freedom to choose between good and evil, and their population is extremely diverse. While many of those who come in contact with humans are in fact evil, that's not always a forgone conclusion. *Qareens* are among the more common evil jinn. They are satans assigned to humans who whisper evil suggestions and bring out the worst in human nature. Every human has a qareen specifically assigned to them. Other evil jinn include demons in the assembly of darkness and those in the army of the first satan, whom Allah has definitively cursed. There are also evil jinn of magic and sorcery, as well as those who enter the bodies of animals and humans, leaving them possessed.

On the other end of the spectrum are the jinn who embrace Islam—Muslims who love Allah and righteousness. These are beautiful creatures, and they exercise their talents to oppose evil in the realm of the unseen—like their human counterparts in the natural realm. This was the foundation of Samaa's upbringing, and though she wasn't living the life of a practicing Muslim, she hadn't completely left it behind. She was a decent and respectful jinni, trying to figure out life and find her way. She couldn't imagine ever living up to the standard of Hakeem though she admired him greatly and detested evil as much as he did. She loved the structure and etiquette that Islam provided, but her faith had suffered a setback more than 150 years earlier.

As a youngster, Samaa had been surrounded by love and had led a sheltered life in the woods with her aunt and uncle. Her family was of noble lineage from the category of jinn whose physical forms are most similar to humans— quite different from shapeshifters or the jinn who resemble animals. Hakeem provided her with an environment that allowed her to flourish, and Samaa had everything she ever wanted—except her parents.

She never knew her parents and had never even heard their stories because no one talked about them. They were a secret that everyone seemed to want to protect her from. But she wanted to know them and be with them. In her youth, Hakeem always stressed the importance of prayer, insisting that Allah answers the prayers of the believers. So that's what she did. Night after night, for decades, Samaa prayed for the Lord to return her parents, but they never showed. The disappointment broke her spirit. It felt like Allah was ignoring her or had forgotten her. So she stopped praying.

Now, more than a century later, Sulaiman and his prayers were calling her back to the days of her childhood, forcing her to reconsider her relationship with Allah. It was a daunting prospect, further complicated by the fact that she hadn't seen Sulaiman in the two weeks since she had returned home. She was at a spiritual and emotional impasse, confused about how to move forward. With her mind oscillating between childhood lessons and the image of Sulaiman etched into her memory, Samaa wandered deep into the woods to a place that only she had been. She quieted her mind—listening to her soul—and for the first time in a long while, she called out to the Lord for guidance.

"Oh Allah, Most Merciful and Gracious. I failed to maintain the worship You deserve and I'm begging You to forgive me. Though I've struggled to establish my relationship with You, I know You exist; and I have never disbelieved. Dear Lord, help me and make me better. My parents never came back, even though I prayed as hard as I could … and I never understood why. But now I find in myself a new prayer—one that makes me hope again. Oh Creator of men and jinn, I have seen your servant Sulaiman and the way he cries out to You. I have listened to his heartbeat calling your name. Teach me how to pray like him and show me how you answer prayers. Help me understand what I'm supposed to do and give me a sign that points me in the right direction. Also Lord, please make a way for me to see him again."

CHAPTER FIVE

Sulaiman pulled into the driveway after an exhausting day of work. He turned off the engine and reclined the back of his seat to relax his eyes and decompress. He loved working as a consultant, but major projects were emotionally consuming, and today was an extremely long day. On the way inside, he didn't bother stopping for the mail or picking up the newspaper delivery from the front lawn. He opened the door, placed his briefcase on the stairs, and kicked his feet up on the sofa. All he wanted at the moment was to relax.

Half an hour later, he pulled himself up to get started on dinner. He noticed on the way to the kitchen that another real estate agent left his business card on the counter. There was still a decent amount of interest from buyers, though the Romero family was no longer among them. Their encounter with Samaa in the closet was a deal breaker, and it had sparked rumors that the house was haunted.

The table was set, as the sweet aroma of candied yams permeated the air. This would have been a wonderful meal to share with his wife and daughter, but as usual, dinner alone amplified their absence. Sulaiman enjoyed the meal as he reminisced of happier times with his family, when Nejimah was a little girl. He recalled a fun game of hide-and-seek they played, which ultimately directed his thoughts to the Romero boys. He remained curious about the mysterious incident, though nothing ever materialized. As far as Sulaiman could tell, there were no signs of anything abnormal.

Placing his napkin on the table beside the empty plate, the perplexed homeowner walked upstairs and down the hall into the guest bedroom. He opened the closet where the incident was supposed to have happened and looked inside. It was as mundane as a closet should be. Still, he wondered what might have happened that day. Taking a seat on the carpet, Sulaiman stared into the closet as if somehow he could inspect for jinn with his naked eye. It was all so peculiar, seeing that the strange phenomena never seemed to happen when he was home—or in all the years prior to this one. He eventually retired to his bedroom, where he showered and commenced with his nightly routine before bed. The long day had taken its toll, and as the dreamer plopped into bed, his eyelids hammered shut.

Moments later he saw himself, in a dream, arise from bed and proceed down the hall to the guest room. Like before, he opened the closet and there was nothing there.

His chest expanded as he saw himself close his eyes and raise his hands to the sky. Then, in a commanding voice he proclaimed, "In the name of Allah, if there is a satan in this closet, show yourself!" Nothing happened. Again, he closed his eyes and commanded, "If there is anything evil, of any kind, show yourself and be removed in the name of Allah." Still nothing happened. Finally, Sulaiman's subconscious turned his attention to the Lord, petitioning Allah for a resolution: "Oh Allah, if there is a being of any kind that has caused a disturbance my home, please reveal it to me." With that, the interior of the closet transformed into a wormhole, which opened into the midnight sky.

With one hand clenching the closet doorknob and the other secured against the threshold moulding, Sulaiman leaned his head into the closet for a better view. In silent wonderment, he peered into the night sky filled with the most beautiful stars above him. Then, he looked below and saw a wooded area, not unlike those located on the outskirts of the city. As his vision adjusted to the darkness of night, he could see the ground fifty feet below. Upon it were three living beings that he couldn't make out from that distance. He could, however, determine that they were alive; because they emitted a glow, which allowed him to see them moving about.

Sulaiman jumped into the wormhole and began falling to the ground, but as he neared the earth's surface, his subconscious slowed to a comfortable landing. *"As Salaamu alaikum,*" he announced, and to his surprise, everything in the dream responded. The stars, the moon, the trees, an owl, and the three beings all replied, "*Wa alaikum Salaam,* dear son of Adam." Then, out came Hakeem to greet him.

"Welcome to our humble abode, my respected brother. To what do I owe this visit?"

"My name is Sulaiman and I live in The Meadows in the city of Eagleton. Where am I now?"

"You're not very far from home. I'm curious as to what brought you here, if you don't mind my asking."

"I don't know exactly, but I may know once I see it. Are you alone here? It looked like there were three of you."

"No. I'm not alone. My wife and niece are with me."

With that, there was a long dead silence. In Islam, it would not be respectful to request to meet someone else's wife. So Sulaiman stood perplexed and defeated. Certainly, there must be a reason he was there, though it appeared he had come to a dead end. Eventually, he thought of another question to ask.

"Have you ever seen me before?"

"Yes."

"And have you ever been inside my home?"

"No, I'm afraid I haven't. Is there a problem?"

"Well not exactly, but … yes, I guess there is a bit of a problem. I believe that someone has been entering my home without permission. I originally thought it was a satan; now I'm not sure."

"So what's the problem?"

"Whoever it was, they caused fear in the hearts of children, and I'm trying to find out what happened."

"And what are your intentions when you find the culprit?"

"I have no intentions, only questions. If something's happening in my home, I'd like to understand what it is. Why was my house chosen, and who would frighten children, if not an evil one?"

Hakeem summoned his niece, who slowly came forward and stood next to him. Sulaiman took one look at her and declared, "*SubhanAllah*, it's you! I saw you in my dream three nights in a row. It was you in the closet, wasn't it?" Samaa remained silent, which Sulaiman interpreted as an admission of guilt. "But why?" he questioned. "I don't understand what this is all about."

Sulaiman presented Hakeem with an impassioned commentary, detailing the backlash from Samaa's actions. He sounded upset as Samaa stood silently staring at the ground. With her head slightly bowed and her hands folded at the waist, the jinni listened to the dreamer speak, all the while marveling at his presence before her. Were it anyone else, she might have been embarrassed—even defensive—but not with him. The only uneasiness she felt was at the thought of what she would do once he was done talking. What should she say—and how could she prolong this night?

Hakeem interjected with an apology and offered to pay any damages. Sulaiman countered that the noble gesture was unnecessary. He wasn't interested in having anyone penalized or even inconvenienced. This visit was about expunging the heaviness in his heart and clarifying the confusion surrounding his home. Now that he had spoken his piece, he worried that he'd made the family of jinn uncomfortable. He politely excused himself and turned to walk away.

As the dreamer lifted off the ground—ascending toward the wormhole—Samaa felt an overwhelming sense of panic come over her. She was no longer allowed inside his home and wasn't ready to see him disappear forever. This night was unquestionably the answer to her prayer, and in a matter of seconds the barrier between them would permanently be sealed. It was her one and only chance to say something, but she had no idea what that should be. Sulaiman stood at the portal, taking a final look at the breathtaking view. As he turned to enter the wormhole, Samaa screamed, "Sulaiman, NO!" Immediately he stopped and turned toward the sound of her voice.

This was a defining moment—one he needed to handle delicately, and with the utmost care and respect. Sulaiman returned to the ground, acutely aware of every detail in his surroundings. By now, Sakina had emerged from the foliage to join her family. She stood behind Samaa, rubbing her shoulders for comfort and support. The night was completely quiet, as the unexpected outburst had caught everyone by surprise.

Sulaiman's first thought was that she called him by name, though he knew absolutely nothing about her. Beyond that, he was impressed by her daring. He sensed a unique strength and determination emanating from beneath her silent, shy exterior. For the first time, Samaa had truly caught the dreamer's attention. He approached Hakeem with an extended hand and the Muslim brothers shook— each enveloping the other's right hand in a sandwich between both of his own. Then Sulaiman addressed his elder with a title showing respect.

"*Ya Sheikh,* may I sit?"

The males lowered themselves to the leaves beneath them, sitting on the ground face to face. Neither one let go of the other's hand. Sakina and Samaa sat off to the side, close enough to hear the conversation. Sulaiman continued: "Please forgive my intrusion at this late hour. I am humbled by your patience in the face of my own impatience, and by your willingness to rectify a problem that never existed. In my ignorance, I misinterpreted events that were beyond my capacity to comprehend, and for that, I have caused this unnecessary disturbance. Please accept my apology and an open invitation into my home—for you and your family. Furthermore, I humbly ask that you not reprimand your niece for my misunderstanding and forward to her my sincere apology."

Hakeem glanced at his family, who were equally impressed by the human sitting in their presence. He could read on their faces everything they felt. Samaa was nervous and refused to make eye contact. She held her aunt's hand, fidgeting with her fingers. Sakina, on the other hand, looked into her husband's eyes as if to speak on Samaa's behalf. Her silent endorsement urged Hakeem, as if to say, "It's your turn, honey." Hakeem turned back to Sulaiman, offering his reply.

"Young man, we are honored to have you here, and you are welcome at this hour, or any other. We too apologize for any misunderstanding on our part. We ask Allah to bless you for your courtesy and noble manners, which we estimate to be among the very best."

"Thank you, sir. May I ask your name?"

"My name is Hakeem. You and I are members in the same community; I recognize you from the masjid where we both pray. May Allah reward you for your contribution in supporting our new Muslims, and may He bless you on this night of nights, in which we find ourselves amazed. It is a rare occasion for one of your kind to perceive what you have in our midst, and an equally unique experience for us, meeting someone like you. In 850 years, I have never shaken hands with one of the sons of Adam, and yet here we are."

"Indeed. Here we are."

"So welcome to you, Brother Sulaiman. Make yourself comfortable. For you are among your brothers and sisters in Islam."

"*Alhamdulillah* for your hospitality, Ya Sheikh."

"This night is a gift from the abundant gifts of Allah. He is the best of planners; He, alone, knows the specifics of why you're here. Yet what is decidedly apparent is that the destiny of your visit is in some way tied to my niece. So I give you permission to speak with her, in my presence, and I caution you: fear Allah. Know that He is watching, and conduct yourself with that in mind. My advice to her is double that of my advice to you."

Sulaiman turned and greeted the jinni he had once perceived to be a woman. She acknowledged his courtesy with a bashful smile and a genteel reply. As he moved closer to initiate a conversation, Sakina traded places with him— joining her husband and allowing her niece a hint of privacy.

"What's your name?" Sulaiman asked.

"I'm Samaa."

"I beg your pardon?"

"My name is Samaa."

"Oh *MashaAllah* … what a beautiful name. I don't think I've ever heard it before. It fits you though—very unique."

"Thank you."

"Samaa, please allow me to apologize for earlier, for causing a scene in front of your family."

Until now, Samaa had yet to look him in the eye.

Though she was not normally a shy individual, something about Sulaiman made her feel exposed. Ever since the night she realized he could see her, it was difficult for her to make eye contact. It embarrassed her that he knew she watched him sleep; and her attraction for him compounded the feeling of awkwardness. Still, one thing was certain: if anyone needed to apologize, it wasn't Sulaiman. Samaa lifted her head, summoning the courage to look him in the eye. Then, she leaned forward and whispered, "We both know that you're being nice and you've done nothing that warrants an apology … but thank you."

A soft chuckle exhaled through his nostrils as Sulaiman smiled, acknowledging her assertion. "You're welcome," he confessed.

Seeing his smile helped her relax. It was almost as peaceful as watching him sleep, but better. He had an adorable smile that made her feel playful and close to him. As they became more acquainted, she studied his face, enjoying the way it shared his emotions. The longer he talked, the more comfortable she felt in his presence, and she began to break away from her shyness.

Samaa's experience with humans was limited, and she had never actually paid attention to their appearance. So every moment with Sulaiman was a new discovery; there was no one more beautiful in her eyes. He was a strong man with good genes and a handsome face—but it was his beautiful heart that made every part of him beautiful to her. Moreover, he was the only male—among men or jinn—who made Samaa feel as safe and comfortable as her uncle. Something about this man brought out the best in her, and being in his presence felt like home.

The dreamer was equally enamored at the stunning beauty before his eyes. Samaa's appearance was far more complex than a mere floating hologram of a woman. She was a rare vision, the likes of which he had never seen; her physical being was dynamic, with subtle changes to its appearance from one moment to the next.

The exterior of her being was ultratranslucent and shimmered in the moonlight. Then there were the rainbows. In different parts of her face (and especially in her eyes) rainbows drifted back and forth, like screensavers on an old computer screen. They were akin to the rainbows in a small puddle of water, or those floating in soap bubbles that children blow into the air. When she looked at Sulaiman, her eyes sparkled. So he studied them, familiarizing himself with the subtleties of her uniqueness. He had the distinct feeling that, with time and practice, he might someday learn to truly perceive the complexity of her beauty.

"What are you looking at?" she quipped with a hint of playful banter.

"Your eyes."

"And what about them?"

"They sparkle when you look at me. Is that all the time, or is it me?"

"Whoa ..." she countered, blushing as she sidestepped the question, "and wouldn't you like to know the answer to that question? What about you? What makes your eyes sparkle?"

"I don't know … lots of things. I love to reflect on the beauty of Allah's creation. I love the sight of birds in flight, I love the beauty of a flower garden, and tonight, I discovered yet another one of Allah's extraordinarily beautiful creations."

Samaa blushed again.

Then he asked if she was comfortable talking about what had happened earlier. He wanted to know why she called him back from the portal.

"Something inside wouldn't let me stay quiet any longer," she explained. "After everything that happened, you were finally here, in my world. Yet as quickly as you appeared, you were vanishing, and that didn't feel right. I wasn't ready to say goodbye without ever having an opportunity to say hello." Then she narrated the story of how their paths first crossed and all that ensued thereafter.

She applauded Sulaiman's integrity and his love for Allah. For he was the same man behind closed doors as in public. In many ways, he reminded her of Hakeem: good-natured, even-tempered, and having a similar personality. But it was more than that—Sulaiman felt familiar to her. It was like she recognized him within her soul, and that was the impetus for her curiosity—pure and simple curiosity. That's all it was … harmless. There was never any indecency in her motives. Still, she was sorry for trespassing, and she apologized for it.

Samaa continued her story with the dreamer hanging on every word. She spoke openly and passionately about her family, her childhood, her faith, her fears, and whatever else came to mind. There was a clear connection between them as her story resonated with him. In that way, she felt familiar to him too.

Sulaiman was intrigued by her intuitive insights and rational perspective. He was also flattered by Samaa's description of his character. The jinni was an extraordinary being who impressed him in every way, but one thing didn't add up. Where was her relationship with Allah? She was obviously raised with Islamic values, and in her mannerisms were all the signs of a practicing Muslim. Yet she was not. Inside, she was stuck in a place of doubt and uncertainty, and Sulaiman was concerned for her. Then he had an epiphany.

Combing through his memory of all that Samaa conveyed, Sulaiman arrived at a definitive conclusion: the dreams were not for him, they were for her. Three consecutive nights (in the same dream), the sound of his heartbeat had consumed her, only to confront her with an invitation to return to her faith. And again—in the dream tonight—Sulaiman's presence in her world had nothing to do with the Romeros or the sale of his home. It was all for Samaa. The Lord was reminding her of His unlimited ability to answer prayers. If her faith was shaken because her parents never returned, then it should be restored by the immediacy with which Allah had answered her most recent prayer. She had prayed to see Sulaiman again, and he was dropped out of the sky in front of her home.

It was an astounding revelation Sulaiman couldn't wait to share, but as soon as he opened his mouth, everything stopped. He was silenced by a spine-chilling screech that tore across the sky, piercing everyone's ears. Suddenly, his eyes were forced open and he found himself back in bed. He was pulled from his dream by the screech of an alarm, notifying him it was time to pray *Fajr*.

CHAPTER SIX

It was Friday and Sulaiman took the workday off to attend the congregational *Jumuah* prayer. He felt surprisingly well rested, considering his subconscious was awake all night. He and Samaa had literally spent the entire night talking, yet his body was completely rejuvenated with a full night's sleep. It was yet another blessing of Sulaiman's gifted dreams. However, he questioned whether to consider it a dream, since it had actually happened, albeit in a different dimension.

Samaa had instantly taken the spotlight in Sulaiman's mind, as he could hardly stay focused on anything else. Intermittent thoughts of her interrupted his normal routine, but it was a welcomed interruption. Everything about the jinni fascinated him, and he caught himself smiling randomly throughout the morning. He wondered if he'd have a chance to see her again, or if the bridge between their worlds had already closed. He was certainly hoping for the former.

There were only a few cars in the parking lot as Sulaiman pulled up to the masjid for Jumuah prayer. He arrived early to take his usual spot in the front row, behind the imam. As he got situated, he surveyed the grand hall, wondering if Hakeem was there too. He looked for places he thought a jinni might be and wondered how many Muslim jinn there were in the community. Minutes later, the imam ascended the short flight of stairs to the pulpit and began delivering the sermon.

Ironically, the message was about dreams and the Qadr of Allah. The imam reminded his community that every element of destiny is in the hands of Almighty God; as believers, it is our duty to embrace that destiny and to know that Allah has not misplaced or mishandled the details of our lives. Our unique situations are meticulously planned and are specifically designed for us. It was a poignant reminder for the dreamer, and he stayed in the masjid long after the congregation left, thanking Allah for the abundant gifts bestowed upon him.

That night, as Sulaiman slipped into his subconscious, Hakeem and Samaa appeared before him. He had returned to the woods where they lived and sat with them, exchanging pleasantries. Hakeem confirmed that he had also been in the masjid for Jumuah, and he could tell that Sulaiman was looking for him. They recapped highlights from the sermon, enjoying each other's company, as Samaa sat across from them. She was in awe of how similar they were—even though they were from separate worlds.

The elder jinni shared an overview of his family heritage and how his grandfather had embraced Islam. Then he spoke of the dimension of the Unseen, demystifying the existence of jinn and other obscurities. Sulaiman was extremely impressed. He was grateful for the lesson and thoroughly enjoyed the companionship. Then he shared with the jinn a portion of his own story, telling how he had embraced Islam as a teenager and its impact on his life. He beamed when he spoke of his beloved daughter, Nejimah—and almost cried telling the story of the plane crash that took his wife. Sulaiman's was a powerful testimony, and Hakeem enjoyed listening to him. But he eventually stepped away, allowing Samaa to have a moment with their guest.

They sat side by side on an old trunk from a fallen tree, silent at first. Sulaiman gazed up at the night sky, which was as beautiful as the previous night, soaking in the wonder of the moment. He breathed in a sigh and held it for a second, then exhaled. Samaa sat staring at him the whole time, hands resting beneath her legs atop the tree trunk. She finally decided to break the silence, by stating her age, oddly enough. She was almost two hundred years old.

The shocking news caught the dreamer off guard. It was difficult to fathom that she was four times his age but appeared younger than he. His incredulous wide eyes alerted her that she should probably have chosen a different ice-breaker.

Samaa swirled from the tree trunk in a dazzling display of motion and headed toward the pond a few feet in front of them. Sulaiman hopped to his feet, following behind her. She proceeded to explain that in relation to her life expectancy, her age was proportionate to a woman in her thirties. "We age slower than you," she explained, "except when we're newborns. During that time we develop more quickly. We also eat less, sleep less, and live longer. Our physical beings are not like human bodies that require heavy maintenance and recuperation. We're the same as you in many ways but very different in many others."

It was an interesting conversation, mostly light-hearted at first. But inevitably the topic turned to Islam. Sulaiman avoided bringing it up because he didn't want to seem overbearing, but Samaa could tell it was on his mind. So she brought it up herself. She started out with simple questions and worked her way up to more philosophical ones. Like that of her uncle, Sulaiman's patience made her feel comfortable asking him anything, and his responses impressed her. But what impressed her more was the way he lit up when he talked about Islam. The passion in his heart and the emotion on his face opened a gateway into the most beautiful parts of his personality. Seeing that took her breath away, and because of it, Samaa poured on the questions. She wasn't even listening to the answers, just admiring the splendor of his passion.

Hakeem wrapped it up earlier than the night before, to ensure that Samaa got some rest. He was also preventing Sulaiman's alarm from entering the dream and screeching through the cosmos. No one wanted a repeat of that discomfort. The dreamer thanked his hosts for an enjoyable evening, and as he faded from sight, he invited them to attend his class the next day.

It was an exciting class with the largest turnout in more than a year. There were a couple of first-timers alongside a handful of nonregulars who hadn't been to class in awhile. Also, Dallas surprised everyone when he showed with his new bride. He had embraced Islam a year ago and moved away to enroll in an Arabic studies program. Everyone was excited to see him, and Sulaiman asked him to share his experiences with the class. Hakeem and Samaa had accepted his invitation and were sitting up front near Sulaiman. It gave them an opportunity to see everyone's faces and to witness the connection he shared with his class. Samaa enjoyed herself immensely and never missed another class.

That night, they all met in Sulaiman's dream and continued the discussion from class. Sulaiman had sensed them in the room that day, and he inquired if they were sitting beside him. Remarkably, he was developing a sense of their presence outside of his dreams. As the robust conversation continued, Sakina joined in, making it a family affair. Like her husband, she was wise and insightful; and though her personality was more subdued, she was eloquent when she decided to speak. The moon traipsed across the sky as they exchanged ideas, until the time had come, yet again, for Sulaiman to disappear.

Night after night, Sulaiman's dreams opened a gateway into the Unseen. He had visited the jinn for months, getting to know them and forming an intimate bond. They enjoyed his company immensely, and he had become a member of their family.

Inevitably the topic of marriage surfaced. It was a conversation long overdue.

In the beginning, Hakeem had exercised leniency due to the obvious extenuating circumstances. But now, Samaa's involvement with the dreamer needed clear parameters. If they had both been jinn (or humans), the parameters would have been established at the outset of the relationship. But with several months behind them, decisions needed to be made, especially since rumors of an engagement were circulating among the jinn.

As destiny would have it, Samaa had recently converted back to Islam, and her guardians had hosted a major celebration. Two dozen jinn were invited and every one of them wondered why the event was scheduled so late at night. Then Sulaiman appeared before them and the reasoning was clear. The rumblings began that Hakeem's niece was engaged to a human—even though they were not. So the time had come to officially define the boundaries of the relationship.

On a crisp, windy night, Hakeem waited with his family, as the dreamer appeared before them. He asked Sulaiman to take a seat and addressed the couple in a sobering authoritative tone.

"I love you both, for the sake of Allah, and Samaa is more like my daughter than a niece. Her protection is my concern and my responsibility, and the ultimate protection is against that which leads to the hellfire. Allah's way is the straight path. The two of you are a male and a female. The guidelines are clear, and obedience to the will of Allah is victory. I don't mean to pressure either of you into something you're not ready for, but if you're going to continue seeing one another, you need to make something official. I can't spend the rest of my life as a chaperone."

Samaa and Sakina sat across from one another wide-eyed and worried. Everyone knew this moment was coming, but no one knew how it would end—not even the dreamer—and the choice was his to make. He was either going to propose marriage or walk away, but that wasn't as simple as it sounded. He wanted to propose, but only Allah knew if marriage was even possible. Even so, he had to take a chance and go for it. Immediately, he stood with a heart-felt reply.

"Ya Sheikh, I've contemplated the prospect of marriage more than you know; and only one reservation causes my delay. Whatever I do ... I do it for the sake of Allah, and I'm worried that my proposal won't count with Him. As I stand here before you, in my subconscious mind, my actual body is asleep. The Prophet has taught us that when the human being sleeps, the pen is lifted and the angels stop recording. That's my only hesitation."

"SubhanAllah," Sakina gasped in dismay.

Sulaiman turned and could see in her eyes that she fully understood his conundrum. Sakina looked up at her husband with questioning eyes. Sulaiman turned back to him as well, but Hakeem didn't have the answer this time, no more than anyone else. On his face was the look of a compassionate realist. He sympathized with the difficulty of the situation, but the reality of the moment was inescapable. Then, the dreamer turned to Samaa. She was as nervous as she had ever been but didn't want to make the situation more difficult. First, she looked at him. Then she looked away. She didn't know what to do with her eyes. So she tried hiding her face in the cradle of her hands, but that didn't feel right either. Finally, Sulaiman had seen enough. There was really only one available option: to speak with his heart. So he did.

"My beloved brother Hakeem, I am requesting your permission to marry your niece, Samaa. I offer this proposal with a sincere commitment in whatever manner Allah deems acceptable—a commitment to honor her, cherish her, provide for her, and protect her to the best of my abilities. I've felt like a part of this family since the very beginning, and Samaa has renewed my heart with a love that I thought could never return. So please, accept my proposal and let us call upon

Allah for guidance with what is proper for a marriage like ours."

Hakeem looked at his niece, whose eyes were nearly bursting from the sockets. Then he turned to Sulaiman and said, "We accept your proposal." Samaa leapt from her place and swirled around the dreamer like the stripe of a candy cane. She squeezed her arms around his neck and couldn't stop laughing. This moment had taken her beyond the clouds.

Over the next few months, the family ironed out the details of the marriage and wedding ceremony. They prayed to Allah for guidance as well as consulting various experts to ensure the best approach. The goal was to create a strong and healthy marriage, where the needs of both parties would be met, without one spouse placing more of a strain on the other. This was the root of a major sticking point for Hakeem. He was concerned with how Samaa would manage to take care of the home.

For Sulaiman, this was a small thing, and he couldn't understand why Hakeem was making it such a big deal. He'd been living alone since Nejimah got married, and even before then, he was doing most of the housework himself. He didn't want his daughter trying to fill her mother's absence by taking care if him. He wanted her focused on her university studies. Besides, what did it matter if Samaa couldn't clean— if she was also not contributing to the mess? That seemed like a fair trade. Still, Hakeem wouldn't budge.

"Listen, Sulaiman, I admire your selflessness, but a marriage is a team. Both team members are required to contribute for the team to be successful. The husband must take care of his wife and the wife must also take care of her husband, albeit in different ways. You know better than I that in the realm of humans, the wife is most often the governor of her home. She organizes it and knows what is needed better than her husband. So, I admonish you: don't ask Samaa to be your wife if she's not going to be a REAL wife. You have to get this figured out before I can approve the wedding."

Sulaiman understood the thoughtful advice, and the brothers decided to put the matter to rest temporarily. They would pray the prayer of *Istikhara* for seven days, asking Allah for a decision. They allowed themselves an additional seven days for contemplation and reflection. Then, in two weeks, they would reconvene with a final resolution to the proposal.

On the seventh night of Sulaiman's prayer of Istikhara, he saw a dream. Samaa was asleep alone in his bed and she was human. It was a mesmerizing scene, as the covers atop her body moved rhythmically along with her peaceful breathing. She was the portrait of tranquility—utterly exquisite and as beautiful a woman as she was a jinni. She had silky smooth skin the color of honey-glazed walnuts and her countenance beamed with a glow.

She arose from the bed and walked into the closet to grab a robe from a hanger. Carefully, she wrapped the garment around every part of her body, covering completely from head to toe. Then she went downstairs and into the kitchen. The dreamer watched inconspicuously as she reached into the cupboard and grabbed two pots. When she emerged from the cupboard, the garment was a bodysuit bearing the likeness of Sulaiman. She cooked several meals and washed the dishes behind herself. Then she returned the suit to the closet and climbed back into bed.

When Hakeem and Sulaiman reconvened, the dreamer came with an abridged proposal. He was uncertain whether it would meet the elder's approval, but it was all he had to offer. He'd spent hours and days praying about it, begging the Lord for His help and guidance. So whatever the decision, Sulaiman was prepared to accept the decree of Allah.

He explained to Hakeem that in his youth, he was diagnosed with sleep apnea—a condition that sometimes causes sleepwalking. Then he described what he saw in his dream and offered his body as a potential solution. If Samaa could somehow use Sulaiman's body while he slept, she could complete certain tasks around the house that require a physical body, thereby satisfying the final stipulation. Hakeem didn't like the idea at all, but as fate would have it, he was given the exact same dream as Sulaiman. They saw this as a sign and agreed to proceed with the marriage.

Before the wedding, Hakeem held an urgent meeting with his niece. He looked her square in the eye as he cautioned with sternness in his voice.

61

"Beloved, I can't express emphatically enough that Allah and your husband are entrusting you with an enormous responsibility in this marriage. I love you both, but I'm extremely worried about you borrowing Sulaiman's body. Sweetie, this is a matter of urgency beyond anything that we've ever encountered; you must be extremely conscientious. In all my years, I have never seen a situation where a jinni entered a human that had a good ending. Do you understand what I'm saying?"

"Yes, Uncle."

"This cannot be a long-term solution. Do your best to learn and adjust quickly. If you use his hand to hold something, get a feel for what his hands are doing and replicate that as best as you can with your own. Practice getting stronger at manipulating physical matter and resolve the need for him to help you this way. I fear this will be a critical issue in your marriage. Pray to Allah and be diligent in this matter. Do you hear me, beloved?"

"Yes, Father."

Samaa had never actually verbalized the words, but they both understood and accepted that he had always been her father. He loved her more than anything and only wanted to see her successful. That emotion was palpable to her in this moment, and she wanted him to know that she would try her level best to never let him down. The next day, Samaa was married to the man of her dreams.

CHAPTER SEVEN

For Samaa, the first years of marriage were like a fairy tale. When she stared into her husband's eyes, time stood still, and when he smiled at her, a breath of fresh air entered her soul. This was happiness unlike anything she had ever experienced. Every day she enjoyed being a part of his world, and every night they shared a remarkable togetherness in hers—where his dreams afforded him full access. The moments they shared in his dreams were her favorites. His vision was clearer there than when he was awake, and the way he stared at her made her feel incredibly beautiful. In her world, she could be completely herself, in every way, and he was right there beside her … seeing her … holding her … loving her.

Sulaiman adored his wife; she cherished the fact that she could feel his love in all the ways he communicated: in his actions, his speech, his patient and warm demeanor. In every way, Samaa could feel how much she was loved. She thought to herself how extraordinary a gift she'd been granted in that her specific prayer was answered—to the letter. How remarkable that Allah saw fit to bring their worlds together, affording her this blessed husband from a completely different dimension. The power of prayer was a topic Sulaiman discussed with great enthusiasm, and Samaa knew all-too-well that their marriage was a testament to what that power could actually achieve.

One night, Samaa lay snuggled beside her husband, watching as he fell asleep. This night began, in every way, like a thousand others. Samaa lay next to Sulaiman as he slipped into a deep state of unconsciousness, knowing they would soon be face to face inside his dreams.

There was a serenity about Sulaiman in these moments, and his beloved spouse surrendered her undivided attention, watching his metabolism slow. As the peacefulness of rest covered her husband's body, Samaa was captivated by the incredible piece of flesh beneath his breast-plate—the only part of him left vibrantly alive while he slept. The rest of his body gradually wound into a minor state of death, making way for the appearance of his subconscious.

She leaned into his neck and inhaled the freshness of his scent, as his body was still warm after a hot shower. This was her haven—that concave corner between a husband's chin and shoulder—tailor-made to the comfort of his wife. Samaa snuggled in his loving embrace, waiting to meet Sulaiman in his dreams.

As she waited, she was surprised by an unusual sound coming from downstairs. She investigated on her own, so as not to interrupt his sleeping pattern. Gliding down the stairwell, Samaa peeked her head into the corner of the wall and through the other side. At first, there was nothing to see, but the sound re-emerged. This time she ascertained that it was laughter. More laughter followed, gradually drawing nearer and becoming more pronounced. Finally, there it was … the nightmare of all nightmares.

The jinni stood frozen in her place. If she were human, her eyes would have filled with tears. She tried to shake it off and refocus, hoping not to see what she presumed to be the case. But a second look confirmed, with certainty, that this would not be a good night for her. By now, the laughter reverberated throughout the entire house, and the happiness was palpable. Yes. Happiness. For this was not the laughter of a spook or anything sinister. Rather, it was the laughter of love, which every lover dreads.

She immediately rushed to the bedroom, where Sulaiman lay in the stillness of sleep, and stood beside the bed staring at him. One look at him lying there—falling deeper into this dream—was just about all she could handle. She couldn't bring herself to come face to face with it. On the other hand, she couldn't fight the urge to see what was happening. She sank her being into the floor and peeked her face just below the drywall in the first-floor ceiling. She only needed a quick glimpse into the living room, and there he was: *her husband!*

He was holding hands and frolicking about with his ex-wife, as if the former couple had never been separated. Samaa tried to remind herself that this was not actually Sulaiman, but the overwhelming feeling inside her was that while his body might be upstairs, his *heart* was unquestionably in the living room with Shifaa.

Sulaiman and Shifaa were engulfed in an attraction for one another, the likes of which Samaa had never seen outside her own marriage. She wanted to look away but somehow couldn't take her eyes off this travesty that tore into her home and ripped into her emotions like the pain of death. Every moment introduced her to more pain than the one before it, and the longer she watched, the more she could feel something inside her breaking. Yet, she forced herself to watch till the very end. This is what she saw:

Sulaiman stared into Shifaa's eyes. In turn, she would bat her eyelashes inviting him to come closer. He tickled her and her laughter was symphonic. He chased her as she ran through their home, giggling and calling for her children, because "Daddy" was trying to catch and tickle her. All seven of their children were alive in this dream, and each one appeared as a different version of Nejimah—six girls and one boy. When Sulaiman caught up to her, he held on to Shifaa like never before. Their hearts were enraptured in a harmonious song of longing for one another. Every time their eyes met was a moment filled with electricity; the love in the air was as vibrant as the full moon hanging audaciously in the midnight sky above their home. She playfully offered him an outstretched hand, and when he reached for it, she quickly pulled it away and teased him for not being fast enough. He grabbed her and swung her around in his arms. Then he tossed her high into the air and she laughed hysterically, falling back into his loving embrace. She leaned into his strong arms and placed her hand in his, and their love continued into the night as they danced the dance of married lovers.

The next morning, Sulaiman was slow to awaken. As he gathered his bearings and cracked his eyes open, the first thing he noticed was the morning light shining brightly through the windows. It dawned on him that he had overslept and missed the time of the morning Fajr prayer.

"AstaghfirAllah!" he groaned, disappointed in himself for the transgression.

He immediately attempted to thrust himself upright in a rush to go wash for prayer, but the effort was summarily halted by a crippling pain in his head and an intense throbbing in his eye. Suddenly, it occurred to him that he was downstairs on the living room floor and not in bed. He was disoriented and in so much pain. It took him several minutes to become fully coherent. When he finally did, he was shocked at what he saw.

The entire first floor was a total wreck. Drawers and cabinets were pulled out all over the kitchen and den and everything was out of place. Trash was on the floor. A chair was flipped over and pushed under the table. The oven was pulled open; he breathed a sigh of relief that at least the gas wasn't turned on. Everything was in disarray and he wondered where Samaa was. There was no sign of her anywhere and absolutely no explanation for what had happened to leave Sulaiman (and their home) in such a state.

When he finally made his way upstairs and looked in the mirror, Sulaiman was even more confused. And his disorientation was quickly transforming into dismay. He had a swollen black eye and a huge knot on the left side of his forehead, which correlated with an excruciating headache. He called for Samaa several times to no avail, becoming increasingly more worried. His mind combed through the moments of the previous evening, retracing the steps that he could remember before falling asleep. Nothing stood out as particularly alarming.

His most recent memory was of Samaa snuggled beside him, after spending a pleasant evening at home together. *So what happened overnight?* he wondered. He didn't remember dreaming of his wife, but it wasn't completely unheard of for him not to remember dreaming some nights. Occasionally, his subconscious would rest along with his body and the couple would have to wait until morning before they saw one another again. Even so, something about this was particularly unsettling.

A part of Sulaiman felt worried for Samaa, but another part of him felt that he should be worried *because* of her.

He opened the medicine cabinet to reach for the Advil and noticed a small jar of facial cream that Shifaa had left behind many years ago. That's when it all came back to him. He remembered his dream of the previous night and knew it was undoubtedly linked to Samaa's disappearance. Sulaiman shouted, demanding that Samaa present herself. Still there was no answer.

On the other side of town, Samaa sat under a tree, breathing heavily. She had rushed from her home, in a panic, for fear of what she had done, violating the trust of her husband and betraying the vows of her marriage. She was nervous and distraught, her emotional equilibrium off kilter. As a result, she struggled to make sense of the events that transpired in Sulaiman's dream—or the wreckage that ensued thereafter. That night, an overwhelming emotional pain had incited a rage within her that she had never experienced. In hindsight, her behavior both embarrassed and frightened her. The question arose in her mind whether this was an evil that had always laid dormant within her—perhaps a sign of the inevitability of the eventual evil of all jinn. No … that wasn't the case! She was not inherently evil, albeit slightly overdramatic. But in light of her reprehensible conduct, she felt less than virtuous.

In the waning hours, her panic had taken her to the only place she could think to go: a valley outside the city where jinn would often congregate. She had come here a few times before and remembered the relaxing atmosphere. There were only a few human residents (sparsely populated throughout the area), which made it a convenient hangout for jinn—particularly those who were easy-going and good-natured. In the past, when Samaa needed to clear her mind, she found solace here. Sometimes life is less complicated when you're in the company of your own kind, and at the moment, "less complicated" was exactly what she needed.

Before her life with Sulaiman, Samaa was rarely in contact with humans; now she lived among them permanently. The lifestyle adjustment was not always easy, but there were no regrets about her marriage. She was head over heels in love with her husband, and her marriage meant everything to her. However, in this moment of confusion, when life was so overwhelming, there was comfort in the nearness and familiarity of others who shared a similar background with her.

The disquieting memories of the previous night streamed on perpetual playback, reminding Samaa of all that she had done—and every reason why. It was the most difficult part of all that she'd suffered. As if the immense heartache wasn't painful enough the first time, she faced the unbearable burden of reliving this immutable nightmare scene by scene. She could see, in her mind's eye, the disgust on her own face as Shifaa disappeared from Sulaiman's dream, and that's when the rant of violence began.

She tore upstairs in a frenzy of rage and climbed into Sulaiman's body as he rested. She jerked him from the bed and dragged him downstairs and into the kitchen, where she commenced with a temper tantrum that left the entire first floor in utter disarray. Normally, when she borrowed her husband's body, Samaa was gentle and deliberate, using extreme caution. However, this time, she was inconsiderate, reckless, and even hostile. She bumped him into walls and doors and slammed his fingers in kitchen drawers. She even walked his face into the pointed corner of an open cabinet door—which could easily have put his eye out. When she was done making a mess, she dropped his unconscious body to the floor, thereupon realizing the magnitude of her actions.

As reality set in and the blindness of rage began to subside, Samaa could feel the onset of a panic attack. She was horrified at the mess she'd created, and her initial inclination was to begin picking things up. Unfortunately, however, there was no way possible for her to undo all that she had done unless she used Sulaiman's body again. She took one look at her husband's compromised frame, lying awkwardly on the floor, and couldn't bring herself to violate his trust again. Sulaiman had willingly surrendered his body as a vessel of support, for his wife and for the success of their marriage. It was an act of love and unrestricted sacrifice, and what Samaa inflicted upon him was the ultimate betrayal of that sacrifice.

Hours later, as she sat in the valley pondering over this dilemma, it dawned on her that Sulaiman would return to his body in excruciating pain. She knew he would look for her— only to find that she deserted him. How many times would he call her name and be ignored by the one who claimed to love him, who vowed to support him, who pleaded with Allah to bestow upon her the blessing of marrying him? Theirs was as unique a marriage as could be found anywhere under the heavens—a divine gift in response to Samaa's prayer. So how could she have done this? It was a betrayal, not only to the man she loved, but to the Endowment and Generosity of Allah. Her soul was heavy with guilt and consumed in shame; the only thought she had was that she needed to get away. She leapt off the ground and burst out of the valley, pushing through the wind at incredible speeds.

Before she knew it, she had traveled more than a thousand miles, crossing borders into three different states. Still, Samaa was no closer to a resolution for the confusion she felt inside. She had no idea what to do, and now she was exhausted. The speed at which she had traveled, and the uneasiness in her spirit, combined to suck the life out of her. Exhaustion and defeat had won; there was nowhere else to run. So she stopped. Then, in a singular quieting moment, she thought of Uncle Hakeem with his sobering voice of wisdom and guidance. She needed the father figure who had been her protecting guide and foundation for her entire life. She needed him now more than ever. With that thought, she mustered the energy to turn back and face the unpleasant reality that she had fled. However, this time, the journey took twice as long—partly due to fatigue, but mainly owing to the trepidation of having to face her uncle and explain what she had done.

CHAPTER EIGHT

amaa arrived back in Eagleton late in the evening. She was undecided as to whether it would be a better idea to meet Hakeem at home, or catch him at the masjid. Her uncle had a passionate reverence for the house of Allah; he would likely not be as hard on her at the masjid as he would in the privacy of his home. Ultimately, she decided on the masjid, but as she approached the vicinity, she began to second-guess her choice.

The nervous jinni meandered outside the fence for several minutes, feeling sick with apprehension. *Why am I so hesitant to enter the masjid?* she thought. Seeing the house of Allah refocused her perspective; suddenly, the looming prospect of Hakeem's disappointment seemed less threatening. It paled in comparison to the prospect of disappointing the Creator. She almost turned around and left in shame, when a silent voice within her cautioned, *"A Muslim deliberately avoiding the masjid is clearly heading in the wrong direction."*

Upon entering the beautifully ornate house of prayer, Samaa made her way into the washroom and then onto the luxurious carpets that line the women's prayer hall. She didn't bother looking for Hakeem; it was clear to her now that he wasn't the one she needed to worry about. She needed to get right with Allah—that had become her objective. It was *His* forgiveness that she needed first and foremost; everything else was secondary.

She stood in prayer with her arms folded across her chest, channeling her focus on the Divine. It was really difficult—almost impossible—with all the things racing through her mind. No matter how hard she tried, she couldn't seem to maintain her concentration. If she left her eyes open, she began mentally tracing the lines in the carpet. When she closed them, her mind wandered aimlessly onto every topic—except the one she was diligently trying to focus on. The feelings of guilt and self-doubt had overwhelmed her, blocking her connection with the Lord and making her feel that her prayers weren't getting through to Him.

Still, Samaa persisted, refusing to give up even though her faith wasn't at its best. She knew that Allah was listening whether it felt like it or not. So she pleaded with the Most Merciful, saying: "Oh Allah, look upon me in accordance with the best of my deeds, and not the worst of them. Open my heart to be better tomorrow than I am today, and give me a chance to make right what I've done wrong. Soften my heart and bring me closer to You, Lord. Restore within me the peace and tranquility of total submission to Your Will, and count me among those whom You have forgiven and with whom You are pleased. Oh my Lord, no one can withhold what you afford. So afford me this … grant me a renewed connection with You … and a new beginning with my husband. Ameen."

After a less-than-stellar visit to the masjid, Samaa scurried off into the woods that she had once called home. Hakeem met her out front and immediately sensed something was wrong. With his customary warmth, he greeted her, purposely refraining from asking any questions.

There was no easy way for Samaa to lead into the topic. So she summoned the courage to dive right in and tell her uncle the entire story. After listening attentively from start to finish, Hakeem was silent … eerily silent. He clasped his fingers together, making a cradle with his hands, and placed them behind his head with his eyes closed. Reclining his head in the cradle of his hands, he let out a deep sigh. Samaa was sitting on the edge of her seat, waiting for him to say something … anything! She had prepared for his anger (and the piercing condemnation that was likely to accompany it), but the silence was killing her. *Why was he so nervous and perplexed*, she wondered. Hakeem always had the answers for every situation, but for the first time in Samaa's life, he was speechless.

The elder jinni shifted back and forth in his seat, from one uncomfortable position to another. He was obviously agitated; he writhed in distress, his mind pregnant with an idea that was not quite ready to be birthed. There was an occasional sigh, appearing to be the emergence of speech, but he was so upset, he simply didn't know what to say. Finally, a cleansing sigh from deep within squeezed its way out into a soft, desperate whisper: "AstaghfirAllah," he proclaimed. "AstaghfirAllah! What have you done, Samaa? This is an enormous misdeed! Oh Allah please forgive us ... please help us! AstaghfirAllah!"

His unfamiliar tone frightened his niece as much as it surprised her. Hakeem, who was a perpetually spirited personality, had become subdued, his every word restrained. A scathing indictment would be easier to endure than this. His tone was demoralizing, almost hopeless. In an attempt to breathe life into the conversation, Samaa optimistically offered a reminder.

"I've worked really hard at my marriage; I've been a good wife up to this point."

"Samaa, why are you here—honestly and sincerely, WHY? What are you hoping to accomplish by coming here, and what is it that you expect me to tell you? Whatever it is, you picked the wrong day and I'm the wrong individual. This is a disaster and I'm not a part of it."

"A disaster? SubhanAllah ... really? You don't think that's a bit of an overstatement?"

"NO! I don't. And the fact that *you do* only confirms that you have no grasp of the gravity of your actions. So, I have a simple suggestion for you: stay away from Sulaiman."

"What? No! He's my husband. Why would you even say that?"

"Go on with your own life and leave him to heal in safety. He can find a human to marry, and you find another."

"Allah forbid!"

"What were you thinking, and why did you marry him in the first place if the vows mean absolutely nothing to you?"

"My marriage means *everything* to me. What are you saying?"

"What are *you doing*? You have physically harmed this man, and he is your husband! You take this marriage as a joke … and marriage is not a small thing, Samaa. My greatest fear for you, right now, is that you fail to realize what this could mean for your soul in the Hereafter."

"You don't think I realize that? I …"

She stopped herself to quiet her mind and soften her tone. She had never been confrontational with Hakeem, and it was unsettling. Her life felt like it was unraveling—spiraling from bad to worse. First with her husband and now her uncle. She closed her eyes, silently begging Allah to rescue her and make this all go away. Then, in a second attempt to change the direction of the conversation, she apologized.

"I'm sorry, Uncle, please forgive me. I came to you because I need you—now more than ever. Every time I've ever needed direction, you guided me … you protected me … you showed me the way. That's what I need from you now. For two hundred years you stayed with me—even when I was away from Islam. Now I'm a Muslim, and that's when you turn your back on me?"

"Listen. You've put me in an extremely uncomfortable position here. I was the one who approved this marriage. I endorsed you. I signed the contract. How am I supposed to answer for this on the day of judgment?"

"I know … I know." Her head sank in shame as she thought of the worst night of her life yet another time. She breathed deeply and laid bare her emotions.

"I despise what I've done, and I'd give anything to take it back. But I also wish you could see what happened through my eyes. I'm not making excuses, but I wish you could see my soul and know that malice has never played a part in any of my actions toward my husband. I love my life with Sulaiman. But it's not always easy living among the Sons of Adam. Sulaiman isn't the problem, but most humans are not like him. I live in a world where I am literally invisible, and on top of that, almost every portrayal of my race is negative and untrue. That makes me feel worthless; it hurts."

"Listen, sweetie, I understand; but—"

"Do you? Really? Because that stuff messes with your mind—your self image. Even with Sulaiman … sometimes I worry that he wishes I was a human. He would never say so, of course, because he's too nice to hurt my feelings, but it bothers me sometimes. I just wanna feel like I'm as important to him as he is to me."

"But why would you think otherwise?"

"I don't know … insecurity, I guess. But that terrible dream … I can't get it out of my head. The way he looked at her … I hated it. If I'm standing directly in front of him, he never looks at me like that. Do you know why? Because he can barely see me. The place where he sees me clearly is in his dreams. That's my safe place, and I couldn't bear seeing her there. He loved her so much, everything about her made his heart feel something, and that was more than I could handle."

"I want you to think about something. You asked Allah for a miracle; and that's what He gave you … a miracle. Those don't come without a unique set of challenges. Extraordinary gifts require extraordinary responsibility. You have to know that."

"OK, so will you help me? I know I can fix this. I don't know how, but I'm gonna make things right in my marriage again. Will you come with me to talk to him?"

"Yes. I'll go. But I need you to understand, I'm not going for you. I'm going for Sulaiman. I'm concerned for him and I want to make sure he's OK. He's my brother and I love him. Besides, I need to apologize and try to repair whatever you've broken in my relationship with him."

Hakeem wrapped his arm around Samaa's shoulders and pulled her toward him, kissing her on the forehead.

Then they gathered their things and headed out of the woods en route to the Sanders residence. As they entered the subdivision, Hakeem had a funny feeling that something was wrong. Then, rounding the corner onto Sprite Meadow, they were stopped in their tracks by an incredible sight. From the corner, they could see angels in the front yard and surrounding the perimeter of Sulaiman's home. These were mighty angels—standing taller than the home itself. They had huge hands and feet; and the feathers on their wings were shimmering like crystals.

"*La hawla wa la quwwata illaa Billah,*" Hakeem uttered nervously. He cautiously proceeded up the street, with Samaa by his side, neither of them knowing what to make of this unimaginable spectacle.

Upon arriving, Hakeem greeted, "As Salaamu alaikum." Then, surveying the majestic beings standing before him, he assessed that they were guardians. None of them looked happy, but some appeared particularly vexed. The two most prominent angels stood guard in the front of the home: one was the leader and the other was the tallest and most ferocious of all the angels. The designated spokesman looked down at Hakeem and replied, "Wa alaikum As-Salaam."

"May we approach and pass through to the home behind you?"

"Who is seeking permission?"

"I am Hakeem, a friend of Sulaiman, and this is his wife, Samaa."

"By the command of Allah, and the request of the owner of this home, you do not have such permission."

Samaa could hardly contain herself. She screamed with urgency, "Why not? I have to get to my husband, and this is my home, too."

The angels did not respond to her, nor did they acknowledge her presence. Hakeem turned toward Samaa, frowning, as a cautionary warning that she needed to settle down. This was a time, more than any other, for her to use self-restraint—and her total silence would be a great place to start. The two jinn backed away and stood in the street, where Hakeem began to pace, contemplating the best course of action. He wondered why an entire encampment of angels was sent to Sulaiman's home. In one regard, it was a positive sign that Sulaiman was alive and healthy. However, it did not appear to be a positive sign for Samaa ... or her marriage.

Still, Hakeem felt that destiny had brought them here for a purpose, and he pondered what that might be. He directed Samaa to rest on the other side of the street while he approached the delegation for a second time:

"Oh majestic creation of Allah, you are a blessed and divine creature...created by the Most Divine: the Supreme Creator who says 'be' and every matter becomes. Nothing can deny what he intends—nor delay it; nothing can encroach beyond what he has permitted. I am truly amazed by the sight before my eyes, and I wonder ... what has caused this home to be so exclusive on this night? Under what conditions might permission be granted for entry? Is there a certain time—or a specific individual who might gain access? Is the owner of this home in good health? Is he not available to receive guests?"

The angel looked down at Hakeem. He smiled, with half a smile, which made his face appear slightly less intense, but no less serious. Then he lowered himself to a more intimate distance from the jinni and responded:

"From one creation of Allah to another, there is no majesty except the majesty of Allah, and pleasantries with words are for those created with hearts that fluctuate back and forth—while we are not such a creation. We are a creation who remain steadfast in obedience to the command of Allah—whether that command be pleasant or punitive. If you consider my creation to be majestic, then that is a credit to the majesty of Allah and owes nothing to my own abilities. So the best greeting is the one you presented in the beginning—and to which we have responded, 'Wa alaikum As-Salaam.' Furthermore, we cannot provide you with an answer to your questions because we have not been given the answers. We don't know a time limit, or a guest list, or any such thing for permission into this home. In truth, we did not come to grant permission—rather to grant protection, and certainly, Allah responds to the caller when he calls upon the Lord for help and protection."

From the angel's response, Hakeem deduced that the delegation was sent as an answer to Sulaiman's prayers, beseeching Allah to protect him against dangers from among the unseen. Samaa had harmed him while he lay defenseless in his sleep. So he petitioned the Highest Court, seeking asylum and protection from the Divine. There was no way Hakeem and Samaa were getting anywhere near Sulaiman, as long as the angels stood watch. So Hakeem backed away—speechless and crestfallen—wondering if he would ever have an opportunity to speak to his friend again.

The angel returned to his full upright position, standing high above the house. Yet, he never took his eyes off Hakeem—who seemed genuinely repentant. He could hear Hakeem quietly mumbling prayers of repentance, hanging his head in sorrowful regret. The depth of the jinni's remorse was as if he, himself, had perpetrated the offense against Sulaiman. The angel knew that wasn't the case.

Hakeem's faith and sincerity stood out as particularly impressive, so the angel summoned him back to the front yard. "Oh Hakeem, I was given permission to show you something." Then the angel transformed molecules of air into an elaborate vision, presenting an image of Sulaiman as vividly as if he were physically in their midst. The vision revealed him searching for Samaa in every room in their home and repeatedly calling her name. Yet she was nowhere to be found. The scene continued for several minutes, until Samaa could hear the sound of Sulaiman's voice from across the street. She immediately perked up—focusing her attention toward the image of her husband. Then, upon catching a glimpse of the angel's revelation, Samaa was overcharged with an emotional outburst that resulted in a cataclysmic crisis.

The epic moment flashed in the blink of an eye, lasting mere nanoseconds. Even so, Hakeem perceived the unfolding of each event as if in super slow motion. He anticipated this moment would yield irrevocable consequences, and he prayed he could react in time to prevent them.

Samaa screamed at the top of her voice, *"Su-lay-maaaan!"* and in that moment, her determination was intractable. Nothing was going to stand in the way of her reaching her husband. She channelled the gamut of her energy into one instantaneous burst which propelled her in the direction of her home. Hakeem simultaneously tried making his way to settle her down, but he wasn't quick enough. Samaa shot across the street like a bolt of lightning. But no sooner had she advanced in that direction, than the tallest angel drew his wing from behind his back.

The wing stretched into the sky, piercing the clouds with a wingtip as sharp as a razor blade, mightier than any substance in the earth's galaxy. Then, as Samaa attempted to breach the protective barrier, he forced his mighty wing down, tearing through the air at the speed of light and violently upholding the forbidden line of defense. Hakeem desperately threw himself in front of Samaa and managed to stop her in her tracks—just as the bladed wing of protection came within inches of taking her life. The force and momentum of the angel's wing carried it deep into the earth, reaching people in graves who died more than a thousand years ago. These people had once led sinful lives, and the stabbing of this wing was an additional punishment for their sins.

Hakeem grappled with Samaa. He had to hold on for dear life, as she was still unwilling to relent. Hearing Sulaiman's voice had triggered something within her that only physical restraints (or death) could quell. The vision of her husband continued to play before her eyes as she lay pinned to the ground by the loving uncle who fought to save her life. She could see Sulaiman, sitting in prayer, with his hands atop his knees, and his right index finger pointed toward the heavens. Then she noticed his eye—it was blackened and badly swollen. She was mortified to see the results of what she'd done. She flailed and squirmed, trying to free herself. She wailed and screamed with every breath. It was unbearable. Why wouldn't they let her go to her husband? Suddenly, she could hear the sweetness of Sulaiman's voice, calling out to Allah.

"Oh Lord, I have married your servant from among the jinn, and she has betrayed me. I afforded a trust that left me vulnerable, and she violated me with an injury that harmed me twofold: upon my flesh and within my heart. Oh Allah, you are the Most Forgiving; and I am in need of your Forgiveness. So I will not withhold my forgiveness from others. However, I seek your protection against all who would harm me. Cover me with safety, secure my vulnerabilities, and shower me with the peace and tranquility that only You can provide. Ameen."

These words, and the resounding impact of Samaa's reality, sent shock waves to her core, leaving every ounce of her being in pain. It physically hurt her to be apart from Sulaiman in these moments, but there was no more ignoring the fact that this calamity was one that she both earned and deserved. Hearing Sulaiman's prayer brought this truth fully into focus, and her mind was suddenly illuminated with a fresh perspective. The distraught female squirmed and bucked, trying to push Hakeem off of her. Then she tried squeezing between the molecules of the concrete beneath her, but that didn't work either. She frowned and winced, struggling in every way possible to free herself. Hakeem's restraint was unbreakable. She was completely overpowered.

Finally, she propped up onto her elbows and stared at the giant angels standing above her. The pain and exhaustion had taken a toll, leaving her with very little fight left, except to cry out in one climactic battle cry, *"Pleeeeaasse!"* She screamed with every fiber of her being. That was all she had left: screaming to express the heartache she felt. She squealed and screeched and snarled and bellowed; nothing could bridle the anguish in the sounds she made. The dogs in every yard were frantic from the sound of her voice. She was even audible to many humans—though not to Sulaiman, who was shielded in the protection of divine mercy. To some, she sounded like a crying dog or a howling wolf; others perceived the sound of her voice as thunder, UFOs, or aliens. The noise was so severe, for the near neighbors, that several calls to the police were made.

Eventually, Samaa relaxed and relented. Hakeem could feel her relaxing and allowed her to sit up. She crossed her legs as she sat in the middle of the street and watched the projected image of her husband. She studied every inch of him, and her spirit longed to have one more chance to be near him, to take care of him. In that moment, she no longer cared about herself. She cared about Sulaiman—his health, his life, his soul, his temperament, his comfort. She closed her eyes and imagined herself caring for her husband—tending to his injuries and erasing all she had previously done. Certainly, good deeds are capable of erasing evil ones, because Allah stated in the Quran:

And establish prayer at both ends of the day and in the early part of the night. Surely good deeds wipe away evil deeds. That is a reminder for the conscientious. (11:114)

Samaa was now on a mission to erase her past transgressions with a newfound selflessness, in addition to the true love that had always been inside her. She began to pray, and in her supplication, she channelled the negative feelings of remorse into positive energy, focusing on helping Sulaiman heal. She visualized herself nursing his bruises and taking his pain away. She pleaded with Allah to make her prayer a reality.

Her concentration was so intense that the image of Sulaiman began emanating within her aura. She had memorized and internalized the angel's presentation until her core could produce the image on its own. It was an amazing sight to behold, and Hakeem stood starstruck as he admired a transformation within his niece that he could never have imagined. Her faith was increasing and her soul was enveloped in gratitude. Suddenly—miraculously—a singular tear crept silently from the corner of her eye and down the side of her face. It was the first liquid tear Hakeem had ever seen a jinni cry. Samaa was actually crying.

The longing for her husband, the Forgiveness of her Creator, and two nights filled with a lifetime of lessons had all combined, and they came pouring out of her eyes in a steady stream of rainbow-colored tears.

Throughout the night, a number of police cars drove past the Sanders residence, due to the litany of complaints called in to the precinct. None of them stopped, however, because all the lights in the house were turned off and everything was quiet. To the human eye, nothing appeared to be out of the ordinary. Still, the complaints persisted for hours. The captain eventually demanded that someone get to the bottom of the situation.

Shortly thereafter, a pair of officers, monitoring the vicinity, answered the captain's call. When they pulled up to the driveway, they noticed what all the other officers saw: nothing suspicious or unusual. Upon exiting their vehicle, the only thing immediately noticeable was the frantic barking of the neighbors' dogs. They were hysterical because of Samaa, even though she had long since stopped screaming. The officers independently walked around both sides of the house, inspecting the exterior and peeking into the backyard fence. Still nothing suspicious. Finally, the driver suggested that this was a wasted trip and they should leave. However, his partner countered in favor of a more thorough inspection of the home, to appease the captain.

Samaa listened quietly from the street, becoming increasingly more agitated with the officers the longer they stayed. While she had no aversion to the police in general, she was concerned that their investigation was becoming more invasive. She feared they would unnecessarily awaken her husband, who was undoubtedly sleeping soundly by now. There was no question that she was the reason for the officers' presence, and she didn't want to be the cause of yet another disturbance in Sulaiman's life. That was a narrative she was desperately seeking to change.

There was nothing Samaa could do to directly prohibit the officers from her home, but if her screams had upended an entire neighborhood, certainly she could come up with something to divert the attention of two humans in her driveway. She scrambled, thinking of ways to forestall them, though the officers were mere paces away from the front door and moving quicker than her nervousness would allow her to formulate a plan.

In desperation, she called out to the leader of the angels and asked him to stop the officers from approaching her home.

Standing high above the rooftop, the angel looked down at Samaa from the corner of his eye. He refused her request, informing her that no command had been issued prohibiting the officers. Samaa persisted, pleading with the angel on behalf of her husband. She petitioned that, in the very least, the angels could crack the door for the police, preventing the need for them to ring the doorbell. When the angels failed to take action or offer a reply, Samaa called out to Allah:"Oh Allah, as a courtesy for my husband and your servant, Sulaiman, who loves you more than anything else: please allow him to remain undisturbed after all that he's been through, and don't cause his wife to be a difficulty in his life. Rather, allow me to be a comfort and a refuge for him."

Immediately, the angel blew a small breath at the door, which unlocked itself and cracked open.

When the cops arrived at the door and saw it cracked, they placed their hands on their weapons, which were holstered at their sides. Quietly, they opened the door and announced themselves, "Meadowdale Police … Is anyone home?" There was no answer. So they turned the light on and announced themselves again. Still, there was no response. The more inquisitive officer decided to go upstairs. As he approached the top of the stairwell, he could hear the sound of Sulaiman snoring. He peeked into the bedroom and saw

Sulaiman sound asleep. There was no miscreant behavior of any kind at this residence, and as far as the police were concerned, the neighbors' complaints were completely unfounded. So they vacated the premises, locking the door on their way out.

As the police car drove away, a feeling of tranquility came over Samaa, and for the first time since leaving her home, she was able to take a deep breath and truly relax. She found comfort in the knowledge that there is no transgression bigger than Allah's ability to forgive it. Moreover, the angel's breath opening the door made her realize that—even in error—our prayers can be answered, if we pray with sincerity in our hearts. This was the first time she had prayed for someone other than herself, since fleeing her home a few days ago. She saw a valuable lesson in that; over the next few days, her prayers were limited—almost exclusively—for Sulaiman, the man she had come to love more than she ever thought possible.

Fully depleted, the exhausted jinni approached the angel with one final request: permission to rest against the tree in her front lawn. Permission was granted. So she reclined into as comfortable a position as she could find. It didn't matter anymore that her home was guarded by angels or that she was prohibited from entering it. In fact, she had come to embrace the idea, because as long as the angels stood watch, she knew that no harm could come to her beloved husband, resting safely inside.

In the waning minutes of the night, Samaa allowed herself to wind down, as she closed her eyes to sleep. For a moment, a hint of nervousness crept in at the thought of seeing Sulaiman again. But she quickly realized that the morning would find a way of resolving itself. Besides, the Destiny of Allah was already written; and in this moment, the best thing she could do—for herself and her marriage—was to get a bit of rest.

CHAPTER NINE

Samaa was awakened by the chirping of songbirds announcing the time for Fajr prayer. "Come to prayer," she heard them sing. "Come to success … prayer is better than sleep." She arose from her resting place and scooped the morning dew from blades of grass in order to make *wudhu*. Her initial instinct was to go inside and pray with her husband, but she quickly reconsidered. It didn't seem the most appropriate course of action under the circumstances. A second thought was to go and pray at the masjid; but that too seemed less than optimal. She ultimately decided to pray exactly where she stood—under the tree in her front yard, a mere stone's throw away from where Sulaiman stood inside their home, praying the same prayer.

As much as she wanted to go inside and be near him, she was more concerned with what Sulaiman would want and how best to be a partner in support of him.

Standing in prayer, with her head bowed and arms folded across her chest, it dawned on Samaa that the angels had all disappeared. There was nothing standing in the way of her returning home. A surge of excitement filled her being, momentarily distracting her prayer. However, she quickly recaptured her concentration. Every ounce of her attention was focused on the Most Merciful, He who had lifted her burden, forgiven her sins, and was guiding her every step of the way.

As the sun made its way above the treetops, Samaa could hear Sulaiman rustling about the house in his morning routine. Her spirit leapt with joy from the anticipation of seeing him again, and it was a challenge to fight the urge to rush inside and greet him. She waited for a sign from above, granting her permission to return home, but no such sign came. Still, she waited, praying the whole time. She prayed for Sulaiman to have a successful day at work and for his safety in going and coming. She prayed for all that she could think to ask on his behalf, and then she heard his footsteps coming down the stairs. The jingle of his car keys let her know that he would be bypassing breakfast and heading straight out to a meeting.

She rushed to meet him at the door as he exited. "As Salaamu alaikum, my love," she offered endearingly as he attempted to the lock the door behind him. The surprise of Samaa's greeting startled Sulaiman and he nearly dropped his keys. But he managed to gather himself and offer an apathetic reply: "Wa alaikum salaam."

As Sulaiman proceeded to the car, Samaa followed closely behind him, showering him with thoughtful expressions of love. He was clearly agitated and flustered as he got into the car and placed his briefcase in the passenger's seat beside him. The sleeve of his suit jacket fell from his lap and hung outside the door jamb. Samaa noticed the sleeve and quickly replaced it, preventing it from getting caught in the door. When Sulaiman shut the car door, Samaa's arm half disappeared into the car as she stood tidying her husband's suit jacket and fixing his tie beneath the seatbelt, the way he normally did for himself. On a regular day, Samaa would have crawled into the passenger's seat beside her husband, but not today. She repeated her words of love and affection and assured Sulaiman that she would be right there waiting for him upon his return.

A smile graced her face as she rehearsed the interaction in her mind, evaluating whether she had truly been as considerate and attentive as she had hoped to be. It was a wonderful exchange, she thought; she was quite proud of herself. For a few brief moments, Samaa had placed more emphasis on Sulaiman's feelings and needs, and less emphasis on her own. Of course, he was still upset with her about the other night, but this was a great first step in the right direction, and she wasn't letting anything dampen her mood. The determination of this jinni was unshakeable. She ignored anything and everything that threatened to derail her objective—especially the animus of the pestilent Kibr.

Like all human beings, Sulaiman was assigned a *qareen*—a satanic whisperer-jinni who continuously pressures the human against becoming the best version of himself. Sulaiman's qareen was called Kibr. Kibr despised Samaa for being married to a human—especially to the human for whom Kibr harbored the most hatred. In addition to Kibr, Sulaiman was often in the presence of angels as well. At any given time, there could be a dozen or more, but there were always at least two—one over his right shoulder and another over his left. These were the recording angels, keeping the ledgers of Sulaiman's good and evil deeds. Samaa had always been able to see when angels or jinn were in the presence of her husband, but there had never been any significant interaction between her and them. A protective barrier had been placed over her marriage in a way that allowed her separation and privacy from the unseen, even though she was one of the unseen herself.

However, something had changed; on the walk from the house to the car that morning, the angels who were present seemed as displeased with Samaa as her husband was, and Kibr's behavior toward her was reprehensible. He was being a terrible bully. He berated her for feeling remorseful, and he cursed at her, saying things like, "You filthy mud-lover. Have some respect for yourself. So, is it true that you love dirt so much now that you're sleeping in the dirt overnight? What's next, are you gonna start bathing in the dirt? Why are you trying so hard to be something that you're not? Stop wasting your life on this piece of filth and stop begging for him to forgive you."

All of this was happening as Samaa walked with Sulaiman to the car, yet she ignored everything except the happiness that she felt in seeing him again. As for Kibr calling her names, none of that mattered to Samaa. Sulaiman was her best friend and the greatest love she had ever known; no evil jinni could ruffle her feathers about the man she loved. She had done a good job that morning and was now on the right track. There was nothing that Kibr, or anyone else, could do to change that. She stood in her front lawn, daydreaming of her husband's return from work—energized, revitalized, and reinvigorated.

Seeing Samaa for the first time since his injuries made for a particularly unsettling drive for Sulaiman that morning. However, he had an important presentation to deliver, so he forced himself to focus on the task at hand; other emotions would have to be worked out in the aftermath. The conference in which he would be delivering his presentation was originally scheduled for the day before, but Sulaiman's injuries, and a trip to the doctor's office, forced the inevitable postponement. This was a planning meeting to discuss a consultation agreement for sensitivity training, requested by the human resources department of a company embattled in a discrimination lawsuit. Sulaiman hated having to reschedule, but the pain medicine his doctor prescribed left him disoriented and in no condition to make his best presentation. Now, after a day of rest and with all his wounds treated, he was prepared to execute one of his most eloquent pitches to an organization that could benefit greatly from his expertise.

Sulaiman exited the elevator on the third floor of the corporate office building and entered the executive conference room. There, he met a team of twenty business leaders and human resource specialists. When he walked in, the first thing everyone noticed was the white bandage over his eye, and he could sense their awkwardness in trying to pay attention without staring. So, with his incredible knack for making people feel at ease—and in his usual comforting tone—he opened with the humorous remark, "Man, when they invited me on that sockeye salmon fishing trip, I didn't realize they were being literal." A few seconds of polite laughter lightened the atmosphere and Sulaiman proceeded with his presentation. He apologized for having to reschedule, and he incorporated his injuries into the topic on the importance of inclusivity in the workplace:

"Every single person is unique. Communication and team building are much more effective when we can 'meet people where they are' and appreciate their unique set of circumstances—without forcing them to assimilate to the cultural precepts, notions or tendencies of the larger group. Inclusivity is acceptance. Moreover, it is appreciation— appreciation and recognition of important differences that make societies and places better when these are appropriately acknowledged.

"The injuries that you see bandaged upon my face are a perfect example. They're related to recurring incidents of sleepwalking, brought on by sleep apnea—a condition that has been a part of my life for years. Thankfully, I had never experienced a dangerous episode before this one—and even this was a fluke occurrence. The important thing to note here is that while my condition may have an impact on my life, it has absolutely zero impact on my ability to perform my job, and to do so at an exceptional level of proficiency. That is what should matter most, and I think most organizations understand that part. However, what gets missed is that this 'exceptional level of proficiency' that I'm talking about is not automatic. If I'm made to feel uncomfortable in the workplace, or required to take on a persona that is inauthentic, then I am far less likely to produce my best work.

"We are all different, and we all bring something unique to the table—but with those unique talents comes a unique set of challenges and opportunities. Differing temperaments and perspectives are as much a part of diversity as the 'variety of talents' we love to talk about. Diversity is a package deal; and inclusivity is making the most of a diverse workforce by coming to terms with—and learning to work effectively with—the entire package."

Sulaiman's presentation was a raging success, and he was able to secure a contract more lucrative than he had originally estimated. His message resonated with the entire team and his authenticity won their hearts. He had illuminated a vision of potential within this company that transcended the particulars of the lawsuit they faced, and he helped their leaders embrace a paradigm shift that would favorably impact their workforce into the foreseeable future.

After his presentation, Sulaiman toured the facilities and spent time becoming acquainted with as many team members as time would allow. He relished the opportunity to spend informal quality time with any team he was training. This was an element of his work about which he was very passionate, as it allowed the training to be fostered by organic relationships with the trainer. The HR team ordered lunch from the Cheesecake Factory and asked if Sulaiman had a favorite meal that they could treat him to. He ordered the barbecue salmon plate and humorously requested, "Please eighty-six the sockeye; I just want the salmon this time." The small group erupted in laughter and continued planning the agenda for the next few weeks of training.

As he started on the drive home, Sulaiman thought to himself that it was good for him to be out of the house today. Working from home was wonderful, but getting out and mingling with other professionals also has its rewards. Plus, it took his mind off his worries and disappointments regarding Samaa. He had actually forgotten about the other night for most of the day, but now on the drive home, he reflected on the events of this morning and how different she seemed. Her energy … her tone … something was clearly different about her now. Obviously, she was struggling with feelings of guilt, but it seemed more than that. Sulaiman couldn't put his finger on it, but whatever was going on with Samaa completely consumed his thoughts as he drove home. What was going on with his wife? He had pieced together that jealousy caused her to hurt him, but he couldn't quite figure out her behavior upon returning this morning. Why was she waiting at the door when she could have just come into the house, and why didn't she get into the car and go along for the ride, as she normally would have? Though it was clear Sulaiman didn't want her along for the ride, it was unlike Samaa not to be persistent and headstrong.

As he pulled up to their home, sure enough there she was—just as promised—waiting outside in the yard. Samaa had seen the car emerge at the end of the block, and she made a point to move away from the tree and come out of the shade. Sulaiman was unable to see his wife in the shade, but if she stood in the sun, he could see her as a blurry image— like the appearance of vapor on the road when looking into the distance, toward the horizon. Samaa wanted her husband to know that she was there for him and that she had been there all day waiting for his return. She didn't know if his meeting would be forty-five minutes or nine hours long, but she waited and was happy to see him. When she saw him squinting in her direction, she knew that he could see her and she wondered what he was thinking. Was he still upset?

Yes, of course, but she hoped there was a chance he would share how his day had gone.

Sulaiman pulled into the driveway and got out of the car. Then, in the same nurturing, repentant voice that Samaa used that morning, she greeted, "As Salaamu alaikum, my love. How was your day?"

"Wa alaikum As-Salaam. Alhamdulillah, it was good."

"Oh Alhamdulillah, that's wonderful. I was praying for that and I'm happy it went well." She followed beside him as he walked to the house and again stopped at the door. "Well, now you can take some time to relax from a job well done. I'm so happy to see you and to know your day was successful."

Sulaiman unlocked the door and proceeded into the home, while Samaa waited—hoping to be invited in, but prepared to stay outside if she wasn't. Again, Sulaiman was baffled by his wife's peculiar behavior. Why didn't she just walk into the house? Usually she would go right through the door before he had a chance to open it. What was going on with her? He started to say something but decided to the contrary. He still hadn't fully gotten over his anger, and, as curious as he was about the way she was acting, if she was going to stay outside, he was going to let her stay outside. He probably needed the additional time alone anyway. So he closed the door behind himself and sat on the bench in the foyer to remove his shoes.

The smell of something cooking was immediately noticeable from the foyer. It was the aroma of his favorite dish. Now he was truly perplexed. What was going on? How was she able to start dinner?

As he walked around the living room and into the kitchen, Sulaiman noticed that some of the things he had left out were now put away. Upon further inspection, he realized that the entire home had been cleaned spotless. He checked one room after the other—all with the same result. Then he stopped to use the restroom and noticed that Samaa had drawn a warm bath for him. Now this was just too much. He didn't know what to think and his mind started roaming through the scenarios that would make it possible for Samaa to accomplish all of this in his absence.

The whole point of her utilizing his body was because physical objects are easier to manipulate with a physical body. So if she didn't use his body to do all of this, how did she get it done? On one hand, Sulaiman's heart was touched by the warm-hearted gesture. However, on the other hand, he was worried about what measures she had to take to accomplish all of this. She wouldn't have dared to use someone else's body … would she? Sulaiman now needed definitive answers to explain what was going on.

"Samaa!!!" he hollered her name. Then, immediately the doorbell rang. "Samaa, I know you hear me. Present yourself!" She rang the doorbell again. "Fine," he relented. "If you want to play this game, I'll play it."

Sulaiman went downstairs and answered the door, knowing that Samaa was the one ringing it. "What's going on? How did you do all of this? Did you use a—"

"AstaghfirAllah!!! I have NEVER EVER possessed a human body and never even entered one before I married you." She was incensed by the suggestion but quickly regained her calmer demeanor as she explained, "Sulaiman, my love, I did not use someone else's body, and I would never do such a thing. Nor do I feel it appropriate to use your body after what I did, but I still have responsibilities as your wife, and I wanted you to come home and be pleased to find it a place of comfort and refuge."

"But the pots and the trash. How did you move them?"

"By the help and permission of Allah."

"And the bathroom faucet … how on earth did you turn the water on?"

Sulaiman was amazed by her diligence. He fully understood how difficult a task it was for her to turn on a water faucet. This was not like mustering the energy to physically hold an object or carry it across the room. No. It was much more difficult than that. For a jinni to loosen a knob that was tightened with human strength would require an enormous use of force and energy. It was almost unbelievable to him. "Did you really do all this by yourself?"

Samaa looked into her husband's eyes and nodded her head, affirming that she had in fact accomplished all of this without any help. With that, she broke down in tears and collapsed onto the floor. Exhausted and overrun with emotion, she had maintained her composure for as long as she could. The last two and a half days left her emotionally spent and sobbing into her folded arms in the middle of the floor. She had given her all to this day. Every ounce of effort within her was spent on trying to right her wrongs and reestablish the connection with her husband that she had lost. Through sheer determination, she had found ways to move physical objects and tackle projects that were normally beyond her capacity to perform. She was relentless and had found a way to get it done.

There was something about Samaa that refused to fail. Something about this jinni made her destined for more than being defined by her mistakes or inabilities. Successfully running the bath water actually took her longer than an hour (and more than a dozen attempts), but she wouldn't give up until it worked. There was never a question in her mind that her rightful place was with her husband and that this marriage was a part of her destiny. So she poured everything she had into completing household chores that afternoon— not because of the chores, but because of her love for her husband and her desire to restore the love and trust in their relationship. She had made it her mission to show that no one was more qualified than she to be a wife to her soul mate. Now that the chores were all complete, exhaustion and emotion consumed her.

Sulaiman stood in awe, utterly amazed by all that Samaa had done. He was amazed at her diligence and at her love for him, which was clearly without limit. He was speechless as he tried to make sense of all that had transpired, including the fact that he was seeing her shed tears for the very first time. He had so many questions, but he could see that his wife was completely exhausted and now was not the time for talking. There would be plenty of time for questions later. For now, what mattered is that they were together. That was the key—togetherness. Being with his wife felt as natural to Sulaiman as breathing, and with that thought, he decided to put all else to the side. Any questions or concerns could be addressed on another day; today they were together. This was their crossroads and Samaa was still his choice. So he forgave her, because he never stopped loving her.

Sulaiman sat on the bottom step of the staircase and pulled Samaa up into his lap, where she huddled close to him as if to be hiding from the world around her. This was the only place she wanted to be, and all that she had endured finally seemed worthwhile now that she was home again. Those magical tears of hers (that no one could explain) had not fallen in vain. In her repentance before the Lord and her tireless efforts to be better, Samaa had found a way to erase an evil deed with a good one and to be in the arms of her most beloved, and that was the best medicine for her pain. She buried herself in the sound of his heartbeat until she fell asleep.

CHAPTER TEN

Sulaiman sat at the bottom of the stairs holding his invisible wife, who had fallen asleep in his embrace. Drifting in his mind from one daydream to another, he found himself lost in thought until the beautiful voice, in the athan clock, announced to him the time for Maghreb prayer. He carried Samaa up the steps and gently laid her across the bed before entering the washroom to make wudhu. A few minutes later, he re-emerged with water dripping from his beard. He leaned over the bed to place a gentle kiss on his wife's forehead.

"Come on, love. It's time for prayer."

"OK, I'm coming … wait for me." Samaa made her way to the restroom, where Sulaiman had left a light drip running from the faucet for her to make wudhu. Afterwards, she joined him in prayer, and all was right in the world again.

That night, Sulaiman did not have a dream. Rather, the couple slept the entire night, which afforded Samaa her much-needed rest. She had never slept an entire night in her life, but she had never needed this much rest before. The next morning, they arose for prayer; immediately thereafter, Samaa headed into the kitchen, but Sulaiman called her back.

"Where are you going?"

"Nowhere, just getting started with your breakfast."

"No you're not. How are you planning to do that—by yourself? No, Samaa. I don't want you overworking the way you did yesterday. There's no need for that."

"Sulaiman, I don't mind. Besides, I want to." Samaa glided over to her husband and kissed his eye beneath the gauze pad which covered it.

"I understand that, sweetheart, but I'm asking you to hold off for now, OK? We've both had a lot to deal with, and I just want to relax for now. Cooking and chores will always be there, OK? Not now."

"OK my love, I won't do it if you don't want me to, but what are you gonna to eat?"

"I'm fine. I'll grab a bagel and a bowl of cereal today. Actually, you know what? I've got a better idea. Let's spend the day together and do something fun. I don't have to get started on my training plan right away. I can start on it tomorrow."

A day together sounded like a wonderful idea. Samaa could hardly contain her excitement. She smiled as wide as her face would allow, and surprisingly, Sulaiman could see it. He pointed at her face and started laughing hysterically. This prompted her laughter as well—though she wasn't quite sure what they were laughing about. So he leaned in close to her and explained, "You're never gonna believe this, but I can see your smile."

She gasped in disbelief, "Really!"

"Yes, and it is as beautiful as in my dreams."

Something was happening in their marriage, and they could both feel it. Last night, for the first time, he saw real tears in her eyes. Now he could see her smile as clearly as anything else in the room. Neither of them could know the full implications of the latest developments in their dynamic, but being back together was fulfillment enough, without needing to have an answer for everything that was happening.

They spent an incredible day together—as perfect a day as any normal day could ever be. They ran errands, exploring a city that they both knew like the back of their own hands. Still, it seemed fresh and new because they were back together, and somehow they were even better than before. Samaa spent most of the day with her hand clasped to the inside of Sulaiman's elbow, like a typical American bride being escorted down the aisle. Their romance and friendship had suddenly progressed far beyond any of their prior expectations, and it appeared that the most devastating problem they faced—the one that threatened to destroy their marriage—had only made them stronger.

Upon returning home, Sulaiman reclined in his favorite chair while Samaa relaxed across from him, stretched out on the sofa. After several minutes of silence, he asked if she would tell him the story of exactly what happened the night of his injuries. She agreed and started from the beginning, telling him all that she saw, the night he dreamed of Shifaa. She spared no detail, except when it came to her reaction, as it made her extremely uncomfortable to think of how poorly she behaved. Sulaiman could sense her discomfort, so he didn't force the issue. He simply listened to all that she was willing to share.

She told him how she had run away and how far she'd gone. Then she described enlisting the help of her uncle and the enormous angels that stood protecting Sulaiman inside their home. Sulaiman was astonished to learn of the angels and he listened intently, hanging on her every word. As she wrapped the story to a close, Samaa reflected on what she considered the most important lessons she'd learned.

"Honestly, Sulaiman, this experience has given me a perspective that has changed me forever. When I saw you in the angel's revelation, something happened to me, and I will never be the same. I see you differently now; I admire you differently; and my love for you is different. I have always respected you as an individual and as someone who genuinely loves Allah, but now I respect you as someone whom I presume that Allah loves in return. I find myself wishing to have the relationship with Allah that you have and wanting to be your partner in worshipping Him; most importantly, I don't ever want to be the reason for your pain again. It's unfortunate that I had to learn all of this the hard way, but the lessons are cemented in my psyche forever.

"As for my completing all the chores, I honestly don't know how I did it all. At some point, I was probably just functioning on pure passion or desperation—maybe a little of both. Yesterday was physically the hardest day of my life, and still that was easier than the night before, which was emotionally the hardest night of my life. I heard you ask Allah to protect you from vulnerability, and it shocked my soul. I don't ever want to represent danger, harm, or insecurity of any kind when it comes to you. I want to be your safe place … your friend … your comfort, because these are the things you represent in my life—and always have."

For a moment, Sulaiman sat still, silently mulling over all his wife had shared, and processing the plethora of emotions that it conjured inside of him. Samaa had commented earlier that he was quieter than usual, and she could sense him deep in thought as they walked about the city. She was eager for him to open up, and he finally seemed ready after all that she had shared. Her perspective resonated with him. In Sulaiman's eyes, the two were kindred spirits—more similar in character than he had realized. Listening to the description of her remorse gave him a sense of deja vu, and the time had come for Sulaiman to share with Samaa the full story of how his life with Shifaa had come to an abrupt ending years before.

"My love, words cannot fully express how you've touched me today. Your effort has won my heart and your diligence has earned my forgiveness. In this moment, there is nothing between you and me except love and goodness. There is no stain on my heart involving you; nothing about you displeases me. So rest assured that you are as close to me, and as dear to my heart, as you have ever been. The lessons you have learned are lessons for me as well, and I applaud your willingness to learn them and your humility in doing so. Like you, I am intimately aware of the feelings of guilt and remorse, but the difference between us is that you reacted quickly and responded with *ihsan*. As for me, I failed. I waited and I lost my opportunity. What you saw in my dream was a true picture of my life with Shifaa. That woman was the entire world to me. I knew it then, but I realized it even more once she was gone.

"What everyone knows is that she died in a plane crash, but what they don't know is that she asked me to divorce her—and that's why she was on the plane in the first place. Several months prior, I was considering the idea of marrying a second wife—an idea which seemed quite harmless at the time. It's uncanny how a mind with such intelligence can be so naive; but that was me. I envisioned a scenario wherein my entire family would live happily ever after and my life with Shifaa would be uninterrupted by the addition of another woman who loved me equally. I had begun communicating with someone else, and I decided to ask Shifaa's permission to marry her. It was a catastrophe.

"I never married the second wife, but I didn't have to … the damage was done. First of all, I should have had the conversation with Shifaa before I started communicating with the other woman. But more importantly, a husband has to have a gauge of where his wife is emotionally—where is she most fragile. We went for a walk one night after she saw a letter that I'd written to the other woman. It was painful for me to see how much it hurt her. That was the first time I had an inkling of the impact of my actions on her heart. We held hands, walking in an empty parking lot, and all of a sudden she stopped. She stood there, lifeless—staring into thin air with eyes glazed over. I turned to face her and she looked straight through me. Her head sank in anguish as she whispered, 'But you were my best friend' and collapsed into my arms, crying silent tears upon my shoulder. She was broken.

"I had always perceived that our relationship could withstand anything. Shifaa was the love of my life; it was unthinkable that our marriage could ever be damaged beyond repair. That optimism, however, did not serve me well. I was lackadaisical in my efforts to heal her heart, because I thought it was enough that I had decided not to marry the other woman. A part of me felt that she should be grateful that I chose not to marry a second wife. In my mind, I was doing that for her, seeing that it was my Islamic right to marry again. I was careless and selfish; I never invested the level of desperation, or sense of urgency, that her heart deserved. That selfishness cost me the love of a lifetime. I lost her because I didn't fight for her … until it was too late.

"In hindsight, I wished I had been more like you. Had I screamed and awakened all the neighbors—had I done all the things you were willing to do—I might have won her heart back. But I was stubborn; and for whatever reason, Allah had written a different destiny for me. I wanted you to know this story so you could see that I truly understand what it feels like to hurt the one you love and wish for a second chance to make it right. That life is behind me now; but the lessons have remained and I forgive you, Samaa. I forgive you with every ounce of my heart. I only ask that you be patient with me, as I may sometimes have dreams about her. That's not something I can control, and I'm continuing to grow and learn what love is like without her in my life. Before you came along, I dreamed of her always. So be patient, my love, the best chapter of our love is still ahead."

Sulaiman poured out his emotions—laying them bare for Samaa to see everything inside of him. This was therapy for him—allowing for much needed healing and closure. For Samaa, it endeared her to him even more. She understood him completely and intimately, and she had never felt closer to him than at that moment. They were truly partners now—partners in love and in life, partners in guilt and repentance, partners in understanding that every creature falls short and is in need of the Mercy of Allah.

They continued to chat well into the night, expounding upon their dreams, fears, prayers, and all the things that made them unique as individuals. They also discussed a decision that they both agreed they wanted to change about their marriage. Neither of them felt it was appropriate for Samaa to continue using her husband's body while he slept. While they saw it as a necessary element of their marriage in the early days, they agreed that it presented a dynamic that was no longer aligned with how they wanted their marriage to be defined. They were inspired by the reunion of their hearts and collaborated on ways to accommodate for their physical differences as related to teamwork around the house. Each spouse was fully invested in how to utilize individual strengths in order to maximize the benefit within the marriage. It was a challenge they approached in a manner of making the home handicap-accessible for Samaa. They came up with simple, revolutionary ideas that made housework easier for her. Sulaiman crafted a tailor-made dusting gown made of chiffon. Samaa could wear it like a robe, and it made dusting easier than physically holding a heavy feather duster.

They started getting all the little things right—the day-to-day niceties that strengthen a marriage and a friendship. Their love was in sync and growing stronger with each passing day. Samaa also began to notice that with practice, she grew stronger and no longer required some of the workarounds that they had developed for her. She became extremely comfortable in her home, and there was a strong sense of peace in her life. She adored her husband and their life together. For they had seemingly found the rhyme and rhythm for living happily ever after.

CHAPTER ELEVEN

Over the years, the rumblings that "Mr. Sanders lives in a haunted house" gained momentum throughout the neighborhood, and even though there was no way for anyone to prove it, the attention raised a few eyebrows among prominent community members. Even the mayor seemed keen on getting to know him a little better, and every once in awhile, Sulaiman would oblige with an appearance at a community event that the mayor would be attending. Aside from that, he never paid much attention to everyone's speculation. Besides, even if he told them the truth, no one would understand the nuances of his home life. So he pretended not to hear the gossip and focused instead on being the best neighbor and citizen he could be. His kindness and honesty endeared him to his neighbors, and he was held in high esteem for being pleasant, personable, and always willing to help anyone in need. So the rumors were often thwarted by the simple fact that Sulaiman simply didn't fit the stereotype of an old recluse living in a haunted house.

As for life at home, the loving couple couldn't be happier. They had found a routine in their marriage that allowed them to finish each other's sentences as if they could read one another's minds. They had adapted their extraordinary relationship into as normal a lifestyle as they could ever have hoped. They spent quality time together every day, while the majority of their togetherness continued on in Sulaiman's dreams. The special moments they shared in his subconscious continued for the rest of their lives, and Samaa became quite adept at recognizing the various types of dreams her husband would encounter. She could discern, in advance, whether a particular dream would include her or not. If it didn't, she turned away, ignoring the dream and affording her husband the privacy of his own subconscious. However, there was one dream that piqued her curiosity, and she wanted to do something about it.

Sulaiman's recurring dream alerted his wife after she'd seen the beginning portion more than a dozen times. The dream would come to him two or three times a year, and it was always the same. It began with him standing in a landfill, or a garbage dump, and it ended with him reemerging from a cloud of smoke. This dream was unlike any of Sulaiman's other dreams, which tended to be beautiful visions filled with Islamic symbolism. In some of his dreams, Sulaiman could fly; in others, gifts from heaven would rain down upon him. He often spoke with children in his dreams. Babies who were much too young to talk would deliver the most elaborate revelations and advice to Sulaiman through his subconscious. So in comparison, this dream filled with garbage stood out as an anomaly.

Samaa eventually came to the conclusion that the dream had a specific purpose in Sulaiman's life, and she wanted to help discover what that might be. The next time she noticed the dream, she tried to follow Sulaiman into his subconscious and learn more, but she was cut off by a scene change. Since Sulaiman wasn't actually dreaming of Samaa, she couldn't progress through the scenes with him. She could only see the beginning and the end. However, she noted for the first time that when Sulaiman emerged from the smoke at the end, he was holding something in his hand, though she couldn't discern what it was. This was so unusual, but what Samaa found most peculiar was that her husband never seemed to remember this particular dream—even though he always remembered his dreams. Finally, she decided to enlist the help of her uncle.

The sagacious Hakeem was a frequent guest in the Sanderses' home, as he had maintained a close friendship with Sulaiman over the years. It gave him great joy to see his niece as happy as she was and to witness Islam as a central part of her life. He was impressed by their marriage and often referred to them as the "miracle couple." During one of his visits, Samaa solicited Hakeem's advice with regard to Sulaiman's dream. She believed it to be an important sign for her husband and didn't know where else to turn.

"My soul tells me that this dream should not be ignored, and I feel certain that the landfill is a real place, not just a part of his subconscious. I want to try and find it. Will you help me?"

"Sure, if I can. What does it look like? Can you describe anything about the landscape or other particulars?"

Unfortunately, she could not. All she remembered seeing was trash and dirt trenches at the beginning of the dream and smoke at the end. That wasn't enough information to be helpful. So Hakeem suggested that the next time, she should avoid focusing on Sulaiman and instead try to levitate for a better view of the first scene before it disappeared. Samaa kept that in mind and prayed for guidance, asking Allah to help her find the answers. A few months later, her opportunity came.

When the dream first began, she followed Sulaiman, as usual, until she remembered Hakeem's advice and immediately tried to levitate. Samaa was not one of the more prolific jinn with regard to levitation. She was far more proficient at energy bursts and high-speed propulsion. Under normal circumstances, she could comfortably levitate to a modest fifteen feet. However, this was no normal situation, so she pushed herself to go as high as she possibly could, in order to gain a comprehensive view of the landscape. When she did, there was no mistaking what she saw. Samaa knew exactly where this was. This was not a landfill, and the debris wasn't trash—it was wreckage. This was site of the plane crash where Shifaa had lost her life. When Samaa realized where she was, she lost focus and began falling to the ground. Panicking, she cried out to Allah in fear for her safety. Suddenly, a strong wind blew beneath her, allowing her to regain her equilibrium and reverse levitate slowly to the ground. She wanted to wait and see what was in Sulaiman's hand, but she was too weak from overexertion. So she exited the dream, snuggled beside her husband, and went to sleep.

The next day, Samaa was ready to map out her plan. She had all the information Hakeem would need. Meticulously, she prepared every detail before discussing the topic with her husband, because she knew he would not be enthused with her idea. Sulaiman was a protective husband, and her plan had an inherent element of danger. Even so, she felt strongly that this was something she needed to do. Besides, this wasn't for her, it was for Sulaiman. He was her motivation behind all of this. So she prepared to discuss the matter, contemplating answers for every objection Sulaiman would likely put forward. Then she went to speak with him as he worked in the den.

It was obvious that Samaa wanted something, the way she dawdled at carrying his lunch in. But Sulaiman played coy, allowing her the latitude of an indirect approach to initiating the discussion. She started out asking about dreams in general and eventually got around to the specific dream in question. Her original assumption was correct: he never remembered that dream. So she described as many details as she remembered, trying to spark even a faint recollection in Sulaiman's memory. He listened patiently, but nothing sounded more than vaguely familiar. By now, he was beginning to worry about where this conversation was going. Ultimately, Samaa came to the point of asking permission to travel with Hakeem to Indonesia—the site of the plane crash. She quickly pointed out that her uncle was respected in Muslim communities all over the world, and that he had already established connections with jinn in Indonesia who were willing to help. As expected, Sulaiman was not at all fond of the idea, but Samaa's passion and dedication tugged at him and he didn't have the heart to tell her no. Besides, Hakeem was more than capable of looking after his niece. So Sulaiman granted permission for the journey and supplicated to Allah for his family and their safe return.

Early the next morning, Sulaiman led the family in offering Fajr, and immediately thereafter, the two jinn hastened into the wind, heading west. The long journey would mark the first time Hakeem had traveled this distance in hundreds of years; Samaa had never traveled quite so far. They moved in the wind for several hours, crossing land and sea, until they ultimately arrived in a valley on one of the seventeen thousand islands of Indonesia. This valley seemed immediately familiar to Samaa, as it reminded her of the one on the outskirts of Eagleton where jinn would sometimes congregate. However, on this island, Muslim jinn significantly outnumbered those in the valley back in

Eagleton. This valley wasn't an occasional hangout, it was a bustling marketplace filled with jinn—the vast majority of whom were Muslims.

Samaa tagged along as Hakeem wandered through the crowd, asking around for a jinni named Rumble. One set of directions led to another, until they finally came to a huge jinni whose boisterous laugh was as big as his being. This guy was enormous. He was almost as fat as he was tall, and he was the closest thing Samaa had ever seen to the ridiculous stereotype of "genies" perpetuated by humans. He wasn't a Muslim, but he didn't seem to be a troublemaker either. He was warm and welcoming with Hakeem and respectfully pleasant with Samaa. His laughter was infectious, and what tickled her most was the way his gigantic belly would rumble, like thunder, every time he laughed. She put her hand over her mouth and pretended to cough because she didn't want to be rude and laugh at him, but this guy was hilarious.

The exuberant Rumble led them through the valley and into the outskirts of town, where they were scheduled to meet a sister who had critical information for them. Samaa followed closely behind, admiring the sights of the beautiful island, as the males built an endearing comradery. They soon arrived at a tiny bakery situated in the middle of nowhere. The jolly jinni stood in front of the bakery door, admonishing Hakeem with the last of his many helpful hints for their journey ahead. As Hakeem knocked on the door, he expressed his heartfelt gratitude and they exchanged goodbyes. Then all of a sudden, Rumble let out a giant fart that sounded like an explosion. The wind from it was so strong that it catapulted him all the way back to the valley. As he lifted off the ground, he parted with a final climactic joke: "Uh oh, I think I need to make wudhu after that one … and I'm not even a Muslim. Hahahaha." The echoes of his laughter filled the sky above the valley.

A female answered the door of the bakery, as the two guests tried desperately to compose themselves. Rumble's sheer audacity left them gasping for air in a fit of uncontrollable laughter. After nearly a minute, Hakeem managed to squeeze a proper greeting and introduced himself. The sister was unamused and stood holding the door with a stoic expression on her face. She didn't immediately notice Samaa standing off to the side. She inquired, "Is the sister here with you?" Hakeem replied in the affirmative and signaled to Samaa to come forward. "Oh I didn't see you. Come on in, sweetie."

Samaa entered the bakery and the door was immediately closed behind her. This invitation did not extend to males. While Hakeem waited patiently outside, Samaa followed the sister to a small room in back of the bakery where a table stood with seven tea saucers placed neatly upon it. One saucer held a teacup, while the others were garnished with a weird apparatus, the likes of which Samaa had never seen. The hostess was woman named Lena; she introduced Samaa to five of her closest friends, who were all jinn. They were pleased and quite curious to make Samaa's acquaintance, and they welcomed her with open arms.

The circle of friends gathered and took sitting positions around the table—with Lena sitting in the only chair in the entire bakery. The jinn reclined on molecules of air—each in front of her usual tea saucer—and Samaa was directed to the open space nearest the hostess. A tea kettle sat in the middle of the table with steam rising out of its spout. Lena hoisted it. She looked at Samaa with an endearing smile and poured tea into the apparatus sitting before her. Then continuing around the table, she served each of her friends—pouring the last bit of tea into her own teacup.

The peculiar apparatuses piqued Samaa's curiosity and soon revealed themselves to be a type of steamer that turned the liquid beverages into tea vapor, allowing the jinn to taste and consume their drinks more easily. Samaa had tasted tea hundreds of times, but this time, it was more than a beverage—it was an experience. *Absolutely delicious,* she thought to herself as she wondered how Lena came up with the idea to create such a contraption. There was no doubt that this woman was an expert in jinn culture. She was even more fluid in the company of jinn than Samaa—who now spent most of her days among humans.

A lively discussion facilitated the bonding of sisterhood, as Samaa found herself among kindred spirits. The conversation never felt contrived, and none of the sisters felt like a stranger. It all flowed smoothly and Samaa felt right at home. She could easily have stayed with them all night, but she was on a schedule. She had an abundance of questions without an abundance of time and was eager to speak with Lena privately. However, what Samaa didn't realize was that there was no need for privacy. Everyone in the room knew her story. In fact, being married to a human made her a bit of a celebrity, and all the other sisters had as many questions for her as she had for Lena—though the restraint of politeness held their curiosity at bay.

The intuitive Lena could sense Samaa's anxiousness. She reached under the table and gently cradled Samaa's hand, giving a subtle wink as if to say, *I know what you came for and I promise you won't leave without it.* She had an incredible way of saying nothing at all and still getting an entire message across. The gesture made Samaa feel more at ease, and as the discussion continued, it became clear that Lena had already begun to answer her questions. The artful way in which the savvy hostess navigated the topic allowed her to engage in two separate discourses simultaneously: one with the entire group and another discreetly with Samaa.

The evening passed quickly, and by nightfall Samaa had all the information she could think to ask for. Besides, Hakeem had been waiting now for hours. So she excused herself from the table and bid farewell, while each of her newly acquainted sisters lined up to send her off with a loving embrace. One after another, she thanked them for their hospitality and a most wonderful evening. Then she came to Lena—saving the best for last—and was astonished to see her holding a beautifully wrapped gift in hand. "Give this to your uncle," she said, "and convey my apologies for keeping him waiting so long." It was at this moment Samaa realized why Lena felt so familiar to her. This woman was one of a kind. She had that certain *je ne sais quoi* found in rare human beings like the one with whom Samaa had fallen in love. Yes, that was it. Lena reminded her of Sulaiman. The intuitive mannerisms, warm consideration, and ability to connect with others were very similar to the character traits Samaa witnessed in her husband on a daily basis. She appreciatively accepted the gift and gave Lena a big hug.

While escorting her guest to the front door, Lena admonished that there was another individual who was likely the key to Samaa's entire visit to the island.

"You need to find 'the Hijabi,' sweetie, and that's not going to be easy … not at all. But something tells me she's connected to this. I've given you everything I have to help you. But the real answers to your quest will come from her. You need to be diligent and you need to be careful. She rarely talks to anyone … and never to strangers. She stays in the prairies and savannas on the most remote part of this island. Look for her in the caverns among them. Go south to the mountains and take the passage between them. Beyond the rainforest on the other side is where the savannas begin. I ask Allah to guide your footsteps and keep you safe … both of you. Ameen."

CHAPTER TWELVE

Day two of their journey began much like the first—
with an early start immediately after praying Fajr.
They compared notes one last time to confirm that
Hakeem understood every direction (and warning) Samaa had
received from Lena. The journey south was simple enough,
and when they came to the base of the mountain range, the
passage was clearly visible. There was no evidence that any
human had ever traversed this terrain, but natural phenomena
had carved what appeared to be a wayfarer's trail into the base
of the mountain. As they continued beyond the mountains
into the rainforests, they adhered uncompromisingly to every
detail of Lena's advice.

The two employed vigilance and resilience in every step
of the challenging journey. Their objective was to find an
individual who didn't want to be found in a land as unfamiliar
to them as any on earth. Nevertheless, they persevered.

As the sun approached its zenith, Hakeem suggested
they find a place to rest and prepare for prayer. A short while

later, they came to a small hillside with an opening that led to an underground cavern. A welcoming breeze gushed from the cave and cooled their faces, inviting them to a relaxing siesta from the midday sun. As they entered, they could hear a water source inside and immediately proceeded to quench their thirst. They weren't planning to stay long, but they could both use some rest. First, however, they prayed.

After Dhuhr, Hakeem continued quieting his mind and contemplating upon the Greatness and blessings of Allah. Meanwhile, Samaa exited the cave on a mission to assess their immediate surroundings. She explored the hillside opposite the cavern and was instantly taken aback by the scene before her. She gasped, hardly believing her eyes. She might almost have missed it due to the beauty of the picturesque savannah. However, there was no mistaking—even without all the wreckage—that this was the location in the scene from the dream.

Plush with acres of greenery, the savannah extended as far as the eyes could see, without a single soul in sight. Where to begin the search for the reclusive jinni was anybody's guess, but they had to start somewhere. So Samaa returned to inform Hakeem of her findings.

They strolled in the open grasslands for hours but eventually returned to the cavern empty-handed. By now, Samaa felt guilty for bringing her uncle on a wild-goose chase based on nothing more than a hunch. She was beginning to worry that the answers she sought might not be within Allah's plan. Insisting that her uncle had already done enough, she begged him to stay behind and relax, and to not worry about her. So Hakeem found a comfortable spot to recline, and within minutes had succumbed to fatigue, forcing him into an afternoon nap.

Outside the cave, Samaa sat on the hillside pondering all that had transpired and questioning if this trip had been worth it after all. The sun would be setting in a couple of hours and this was beginning to feel like a wasted day. She had come so far and seen so much; and now in the eleventh hour, her goal seemed to be fading in the distance. Could it really be that she had come all this way for nothing?

As she contemplated her next move, she caught a glimpse of an image shuffling in one of the trees on the savannah. She perked up. Apparently, it was nothing, so she relaxed. When it moved again, she focused her attention like the laser on a hunter's rifle, determined not to look away. Everything inside told her that this was more than a random bird. It was exactly what she'd been waiting for.

After a long wait, she saw a beautiful jinni, dressed in hijab, descending from the tree in reverse levitation. It was a stunning revelation—completely different than what Samaa had envisioned when speaking to Lena the day before. She assumed the nickname "Hijabi" referred to a unique cloaking ability or something metaphorical; never for a moment had she considered she might find a jinni actually wearing hijab like humans. This was unheard of—and totally unnecessary.

Of course, modesty is a requirement of all Muslims, including jinn. However, unlike humans, jinn have the inherent ability to conceal their physical features from the opposite gender. There is no need for outer garments. So why was she dressed this way?

Samaa studied carefully as the jinni motioned gracefully across the savannah—wandering in rhythm with her thoughts and in tune with nature. She seemed at peace in her aloneness, and again, nothing like Samaa had originally envisioned. Based on the description, Samaa expected someone dark and mysterious—not like the sprite she saw before her. Why would this creature need to be a recluse? Her energy was wonderful and there was nothing unappealing about her. It was time to get some answers.

Seizing the opportunity, Samaa started slowly down the hillside and into the savannah. She desperately wanted to speed burst but realized that she might not get a second chance if she scared the Hijabi away. So she cruised along the wind, just above the tall grass. She had closed half the distance between them when she was discovered.

Frantically, the Hijabi exerted an energy burst and sped away—with Samaa in hot pursuit on her trail. Samaa was much faster but not as agile, and the two shot back and forth across the savannah like pinballs—with an abrupt change in direction each time Samaa came close to her. Desperately, Samaa announced she had no ill intent and pleaded with the Hijabi to slow down. The stranger was unrelenting and the pursuit continued, until all of a sudden, they came to a jarring halt.

"Who are you and where have you come from?" the recluse interrogated.

"Alhamdulillah," Samaa proclaimed trying to catch her breath. She was so excited to finally be face to face, that she never bothered answering the question.

They were both extremely tired, but the Hijabi was reluctant to show any sign of weakness. She stood firmly with her shoulders pinned back and her head held high. She exhibited no signs of fatigue apart from heavy breathing through flared nostrils. Samaa, on the other hand, was far less stoic. She was highly enthused and wanted to hug her; however, the sister was standoffish and it didn't seem like a good idea. She was suspicious of Samaa and in every way uneasy—not at all the graceful figure she portrayed moments before, when she suspected she was alone on the savannah. A history of attacks on her life made this jinni cautious about everything and everyone around her, and there was only one reason she had decided to stop for Samaa: curiosity.

The Hijabi initially worried that Samaa might be another imposter; but if she was, she'd be the best one yet. Something about Samaa seemed truly genuine, and there was one unmistakable trait accompanying her that none of the imposters ever possessed. She reminded the Hijabi of someone from her past.

The intensity of the moment began to subside, and as the two jinn continued catching their breath, Samaa introduced herself.

"As Salamu alaikum. My apologies. My name is Samaa."

"Wa alaikum salaam. I'm Nurah … So Samaa, you've come here from the US, I think?"

"Yes."

"From Eagleton, I believe?"

"Yes."

"And you live in The Meadows, correct?"

"Why, yes," Samaa replied incredulously. "All of that is true. How do you know this?"

"Never mind that. What human are you assigned to?"

"I'm not that kind of jinni," Samaa politely objected. "I'm a Muslim, not a whisperer."

"I will ask you once more before I leave you where you stand. What human are you assigned to?"

"I told you, I am NOT assigned to a human, not exactly."

"And what does that mean … 'not exactly'?"

"It means that Allah has not created me for that. I have neither the mission nor the desire to distract humans from their created purpose."

"You're being evasive, Samaa. What's your story? You know what I'm asking."

"Listen Nurah, please understand that I'm not being intentionally deceptive. The particulars of my story are quite unusual and I fear we don't have enough time to give it due justice. However, what I can candidly say is that the road which led me here began as a result of my witnessing the dream of a human."

"Why should you care about the frivolous dreams of humans?"

"Well, first, I don't believe this dream to be frivolous. In fact, I suspect it is laced with a touch of prophecy. Second, this is not some random human. This is my husband."

Nurah stood arrested in bewilderment with eyes as big as moons. "Sulaiman!" she gasped.

"You know my husband?" Samaa retorted.

"Sulaiman Sanders! YOU are married to Sulaiman? You? Sulaiman? SubhanAllah. This is incredible."

By now Samaa was almost offended. "How do you know my husband?"

"I knew it! That scent is unmistakable."

"What scent?"

"You smell like her."

"Like who?"

"Like Shifaa. It's the sweet smell of his cologne in harmony with the gentle fragrance of the oil in his skin. She loved the way that man smells; she wore his shirts when he was away, just to be near him. She carried his scent on her everywhere she went, and now apparently you do too. That's the reason I stopped. Every time you came near me, you reminded me of her, and I had to know why you smell so much like her. Well, now we know."

Then Nurah looked to the sky and supplicated to the Lord: "Oh Allah … your mercy … your mercy, my Lord. It is without limit and I am your servant. Alhamdulillah in every situation and in every time. You are the Most Merciful of those who show mercy and you are the Accepter of Repentance. Accept my repentance and forgive my sins. I have seen with my own eyes today that there is nothing you are incapable of doing and there's no benefit that you would withhold from your believers. I glorify your Majesty and praise your Name, Oh Malik-ul-Mulk."

Then Nurah turned to Samaa and embraced her. She knew exactly why Allah had sent her with the message from the dream. Lena was right, Nurah would be the key to everything. She knew the full interpretation of the dream and she knew the answers to all of Samaa's questions. In fact, Nurah herself was the answer. She promised to tell Samaa the entire story but insisted that she come back the following day, when they would have more time to share all that needed to be shared.

CHAPTER THIRTEEN

A most enchanting welcome is the ballad of songbirds. It headlines the symphony of sounds in nature at the first flush of morning. It's a time when the earth feels fresh and everything and everyone seems happy and ready to take on the day, especially Samaa. When she emerged from the cavern on this intensely humid morning, the first thing she noticed was the blanket of fog covering the savannah. She proceeded to the location where she last met with Nurah and was astounded by the sight before her eyes—it was exactly as she'd seen it more than a dozen times before. She was standing in the final scene of Sulaiman's dream, except she now understood that it wasn't smoke she saw, it was fog. And the individual approaching from the distance wasn't her husband, it was Nurah.

The beautiful hijab-clad jinni emerged gracefully from the fog with her fist tightly curled, protecting whatever she held inside. The two jinn embraced—each one feeling an outpouring of love from the other. They were connected now—more than friends: family. Their incredible day together would begin and end in exactly the same fashion, with a story—one more miraculous and unusual than Samaa had ever heard. As they toured the island under a rising sun, Nurah laid bare the secrets of her past:

"I changed my name to Nurah after embracing Islam several years ago; before that, they called me Umm Lahab. I was ambitious and feisty like the crackling flames of a fire, and no matter how formidable the challenge, I was determined to prove my worth in the assembly of darkness. My mission … was Shifaa. I was her qareen. From the moment she was born until the day she died, I was there by her side—antagonizing every step of the way.

"She and Sulaiman were an incredible couple, and the love between them was beyond impressive. Quite frankly, in those days, it made me sick to my stomach. Nonetheless, everyone could see the pureness of their love for one another and the symmetry in their marriage and friendship. Their family was blessed and their home was filled with *Nur*. She was so in love with that man, and he had such a way with her—with everyone actually. He was patient, sensitive, and convincing. Sulaiman could make you believe almost anything—not because of dishonesty, but because *he* believes. He passionately believes in the ideas he shares; and when he speaks, *you* feel what he feels. It's incredibly compelling—and then … there's his heart. SubhanAllah! That astounding piece of flesh which Allah has created inside of him is something like I've never seen. Sulaiman was my problem. Before Shifaa met him, my mission was easy. So nothing was a higher priority for me than getting rid of him.

"Shifaa was born right here on the islands of Indonesia. Her parents are from Java. They're a good Muslim family, but their mistake was when they separated from her. They sent her to the US with her aunt and uncle to study. But neither of them are firm on Islam, so in America my mission was as easy as pie—until she met Sulaiman. The more time they spent together, the more I felt her slipping away from me. His voice was like music and she would cling to his every word. He narrated stories of the Prophets and the Sahabah, and when he recited the Qur'an for her, it reminded her of the childhood she had with her parents.

"Sulaiman loved talking about Islam, and Shifaa loved listening to whatever he wanted to talk about. They were falling in love and their hearts began to beat in the same rhythm. When he laughed, she laughed; and when he cried, you were certain to find a steady stream of tears flowing from her eyes. One day, he told her the story of how he embraced Islam. His voice trembled with emotion as he squeezed the words from his vocal cords. He praised Allah with gratitude and devotion, and I've never seen a man cry like he cried. When I turned to look at Shifaa, it was as if Sulaiman's tears were pouring from her eyes too. Allah was guiding her back to Islam and there was nothing I could do to stop it.

"Once they were married and Nejimah was born, my mission was on the verge of utter collapse. For years, I watched their love grow stronger as I waited for an opportunity to harm them; unfortunately, my influence had faded. I was stressed and embarrassed because no matter how hard I tried, Allah protected their family from me. I hated them … all of them.

"Then, when I least expected it, there it was right before me—the opportunity of a lifetime. Sulaiman left his email open on the computer, and when Shifaa sat down at the desk, her life was changed forever. He had written a letter to another woman whom he had developed feelings for, and he was considering the decision to marry her as a second wife. I couldn't believe it. A surge of energy rushed through me and I knew that I was back in business. There was no way in a million years I would let this opportunity slip through my fingers. This marriage was as good as ruined and I was certain to claim my prize: instant fame in the assembly of darkness.

"I whispered in Shifaa's ears every night—all night—without fail. I refused to let her sleep, and even when she was awake, she couldn't focus. I ridiculed her, calling her a fool for loving him, and telling her she deserved to be tricked for ever trusting him. I insisted that everything she admired in him was a lie. After awhile, she believed me. I even synchronized efforts with Sulaiman's qareen to ensure my success. As much as I detested that obnoxious, vainglorious Kibr, I needed him. I was desperate—and desperate times

140

call for desperate measures. This opportunity was too big to allow Kibr's arrogance to stand in the way. So I forced myself to work with him. I attacked the marriage from one side while Kibr attacked from the other. It was round the clock work at first, but after a year, we wedged a border between them that disrupted their normal communication, and they were out of sync. The rest began to take care of itself.

"When Nejimah was in her last year of high school, I finally convinced Shifaa that divorce was the best option to reclaim her life. It was perfect. I remember her standing in front of the mirror with puffy eyes and a red nose, emotionally exhausted. Her tear ducts were completely dry and the wound in her heart had scabbed into numbness. It was then that I suggested she go home to her parents. She hardly put up a fight. I had worn her down and she needed a break. She was tired of being confused, angry, hurt, and lost. I had finally won a battle and now I was going for the war—divorce him!

"Sulaiman was mortified. He would have done anything to win her back and save his family. He was weak and heartbroken like a sick puppy, and I loved every minute of it. All the trouble he caused me over the years ... I enjoyed seeing him suffer. He didn't put up a fight when she asked him to divorce her. All he wanted was for her to be happy— even if it meant he couldn't be.

"The day finally came to return home, and Shifaa gathered her bags as the Uber driver waited out front.

Sulaiman offered to drive her to the airport, but she didn't want that. Her heart was ready to turn the page on that chapter of her life, and it was time for a new beginning. Still, Sulaiman got in the car and trailed the Uber to the airport. He parked as quickly as possible and rushed to catch up with her. He reached her just before arriving at a security checkpoint. 'Shifaa!' he pleaded, 'Can I have a few words with you?' She stopped the luggage cart and turned to face him one last time. 'I love you with my whole heart,' he said. 'I always have and I always will. My prayer for you is that you find happiness. I want you to be happy, my love, however you define what that means to you. That is my desire.' Then, with tears in his eyes, he bid her farewell and gave her a gift. It was a golden locket in the shape of a heart with two diamonds inside; on the outside was the inscription 'I will love you forever.'

"He kissed her gently on the forehead as tears poured from the corners of his eyes. Shifaa, on the other hand was expressionless. Her emotions were intentionally set to 'off' as she focused solely on the mechanics of the task at hand. She appeased him momentarily by leaning her forehead toward him, allowing him to kiss it, but her mind was already placing luggage in the bin at the security checkpoint. Sulaiman watched in slow motion as his wife walked away, knowing this would be the last time he would see her but hoping that somehow he might be wrong. He took mental pictures, allowing his eyes to savor the vision of the love of his life one last time.

"I remember having a very peculiar feeling when we boarded the flight. I couldn't put my finger on it at first, but the atmosphere on the plane was abnormally comfortable for me. It was an aura of darkness. When a qareen is assigned to a believer, that is a life of discomfort and hard work, but most of the jinn on this plane looked like they had never worked a day in their lives. That struck me as being unusual, but I shrugged it off as a passing thought and prepared my game plan for Indonesia. As Shifaa got settled in, she closed her eyes and said a short prayer. Then she opened a pocket-sized version of 'Fortification of the Muslim' and read supplications from it. A short while later, she reclined the back of her chair and rested.

"Eighteen hours later, the cabin erupted into a state of total mayhem. Frantic passengers screamed and scrambled as a piece of the aircraft came off and obliterated two of the windows in the back half of the plane. One passenger was sucked from the plane to an instant death, giving the rest a preview of their own mortality. The plane went down, shattering the fuel tank and igniting thousands of gallons of jet fuel. Not a single human life was saved.

"Surprisingly, I had the distinct feeling that this incident was a catastrophe. Normally, I would have relished the loss of so many human lives. I was disoriented and almost lost consciousness multiple times, but somehow I found a way to gather my bearings. What I soon realized was that there were as many casualties among the jinn as the humans, and for the first time in my life, I truly pondered my own existential reality. I watched the Angel of Death collect the souls of men and jinn and it overwhelmed me.

"Suddenly, the memory of Shifaa flashed in front of me like a lightning strike. I could see her in the plane as it went down, rocking back and forth with her eyes clenched tightly. Her closed fists joined across her chest, with one covering the other, as if holding her heart in place. Feverishly she rocked back and forth, praising the name of Allah … over and over again. Then, seconds before impact, she raised her fists to her lips and kissed them. Moments later, she was no more.

"I stood right here, in this savannah, amid the wreckage, with one irrepressible question looming over me: What happened to her? I never saw her soul taken. There was a magnificent flash of light in her seat and her soul just vanished. She disappeared. I have never felt a more unsettling feeling in my life. My mission was summarily halted and I had no closure. Nothing made sense anymore. My life was suddenly and completely without definition. Shifaa was not only my mission, she was the antithesis of me; without her I felt unbalanced. I desperately needed answers.

"My biggest problem in all of this was that I didn't feel like I had accomplished anything. In fact, I was certain that I hadn't. The details were unclear to me, but I knew in my spirit that I had failed. Somehow Shifaa had beaten me. Moreover, her memory haunted me. It was the light … that extraordinary flash of light. I couldn't shake the thought of it. I needed to know what happened to her when the plane crashed.

"Eventually, I came to realize that this tragedy was Shifaa's doorway into martyrdom. She entered that plane carrying the immense burden of a shattered heart, only to find her misfortune compounded by the reality of her imminent death. And through all of that, her faith never wavered. She trusted in Allah and never abandoned her devotion to Him. His name was the very last word she ever spoke. So Allah responded to her and saved her. He saved her from the plane crash, saved her from me, saved her from Malakul Maut. Allah saved her completely. With one flash of miraculous light, her soul was preserved and she entered the Hereafter as a martyr. SubhanAllah. Something happened to me that day. Everything happened to me.

"As I wandered amid the wreckage, I could see the savannah littered with the charred remains of the passengers. Then I came to a small pile of debris and I noticed Shifaa's hand separated from her body—stilled rolled into a fist. There was no charring, bruising, or discoloration of any kind on her hand. It was as if there was somehow still a bit of life left in it. I reached down and unfolded her fingers, revealing the golden locket that Sulaiman had given her. Then I remembered her kissing her hands before the crash and realized that she was actually kissing the locket. She was kissing Sulaiman for the last time. She loved him till the very end.

"I picked up the locket and studied it. In my mind's eye, I could see Sulaiman fighting for his marriage. I remembered how much he loved Shifaa, and their entire relationship played in my mind from the very beginning. I have never felt more like a criminal. A deep remorse resonated within me for the role I played in separating them. Making matters worse was the ringing in my ear. I could hear Sulaiman's voice. He was reciting the Quran as he had done so many times before. In the past, I always ignored him; but not this time. I couldn't help but pay attention as the verses of Surat Al-Rahman pierced my heart, forcing me into submission. These verses of the Quran calling upon the worlds of men and jinn together forced me to truly open my eyes and see what should always have been clear to me. Allah says, 'Everyone upon the earth will perish and only your Lord Himself, will remain forever. So which of the favors of your Lord will you both deny?' After seeing those souls of the jinn taken along with the humans in the plane crash, this struck a chord with me. Then he recited, 'Soon We will be attending to all of you, both classes of prominent beings. So which of the favors of your Lord would you deny? O assembly of jinn and mankind, if you are able to pass beyond the regions of the heavens and the earth, then pass. You will not pass except by authority [from Allah]. So which of the favors of your Lord would you deny?'

"My knees buckled and I fell to the ground helpless in front of Allah and in need of a renovation to my lifestyle.

Allah had guided me to Islam through the very love that I had specifically set out to destroy. I owe Sulaiman and Shifaa everything. Here, take this locket to your husband and tell him that Allah is Most-forgiving, Most Merciful, and he should no longer carry any guilt in relation to his former wife. She had the best possible ending and she passed into the Hereafter with his love in her heart."

The two jinn shared a moment of closure as Samaa extended her hands and Nurah placed Sulaiman's golden locket between them. They marveled at Allah's meticulous design of the destiny of all things. Each of their journeys were interconnected and affected by the other: Nurah, Shifaa, Sulaiman, Samaa, and countless other creatures of Allah. The death of one thing is the birth of another, and the end of one, the beginning of another. Each of them had received the blessed call of Islam, and the relationships between them served as catalysts in their transformational journeys as believers.

Equipped with all the answers for which she had come, Samaa was now eager to return home to her husband. She thanked Nurah for her insight and assistance as the two embraced. Nurah squeezed and held on to Samaa like the memories of a woman she wished she could bring back and see just one more time. For Nurah, Samaa was the embodiment of a chance at redemption. She had lost her chance to make amends with Shifaa, but Sulaiman was still alive, and now accessible. She solicited Samaa with a single impassioned request: to deliver a message. "Dear sister," she urged, "tell your husband that I have embraced Islam … that I have completely changed my life and I am begging for his forgiveness. I don't want to stand in front of my Lord and account for what I have done to him. Ask him to please forgive me."

In that moment, Samaa realized that Sulaiman's dream was never intended as an omen for him. Rather, it was always meant for Nurah. Her prayers of repentance had been accepted by Allah, and He wanted to give her a sign that her Lord was near and that none of her efforts were wasted. The dream was a vehicle through which Allah summoned Samaa on a journey of enlightenment to strengthen her own faith, while simultaneously affording Nurah the opportunity to be fully expunged from her previous sins. Upon realizing this, Samaa was deeply honored to have been chosen for such an assignment. She turned to Nurah and promised to deliver the message, reassuring her that Sulaiman was not the type of man to withhold his forgiveness.

In the waning moments of their time together, Nurah apprised her friend of the anguish she suffered at the hands of the assembly of darkness after embracing Islam. The evil they inflicted upon her was unimaginable. There were more attempts on her life than she cared to remember, but the Almighty had ordained for her to be preserved. As a result of the attacks, she adopted a lifestyle of complete seclusion. Then, in honor of Shifaa, she made two modifications to her life that remained with her forever. First, she changed her name to Nurah, commemorating the glorious flash of light that accompanied Shifaa's disappearance from the plane. Next, she found a way to manipulate molecules of dust and pollen to form her hijab. She fashioned it in the exact same style as Shifaa would wear. This was all to ensure that she would never forget the woman who helped save her soul.

CHAPTER FOURTEEN

agleton had never looked more beautiful than under the sunrise of the fourth morning since Samaa had last seen her beloved husband. Her anticipation mounted as the journey with Hakeem neared its end. They had traveled all night and were only minutes away from Eagleton, The Meadows, and home. She stopped at the front door, taking a moment to acknowledge her uncle and express her gratitude, before rushing in to see Sulaiman. A shower of hugs and kisses greeted her as she entered, and nothing rivaled the emotion of looking into her husband's eyes and knowing with assurance that he missed her as much as she missed him.

Samaa was happy to be home and excited to share all that she had experienced. She took Sulaiman by the hand and led him into the living room, where they sat side by side on the sofa. She described the beauty of the islands of Indonesia and introduced him to everyone she met along the journey. They laughed hysterically as she recapped Rumble's shenanigans. Sulaiman was happy she enjoyed her trip. He could feel her buoyancy and the positive impact of her spending quality time with other jinn. He suggested they plan regular vacations to go back as a couple. She loved the idea.

When the moment felt right, Samaa directed her husband to close his eyes and hold out his hands. First, she kissed his hands; then she placed within them the golden locket that he had given to Shifaa more than a decade before. When he opened his eyes, there was a momentary state of shock. "Where did you get this?" he marveled. There could not have been a more surreal moment—even in a life as extraordinary his.

Sensing his difficulty in processing the moment, Samaa moved closer to him and placed her hands gently upon his cheeks to relax him. She stared into his eyes with her face mere inches away from his. Then she reminded him what an inspiration he had been to so many. She lauded his efforts in always striving to be his best and insisted that Allah would never allow any good deed to go unrewarded. Finally, Samaa recounted every detail of Nurah's story, holding Sulaiman's attention captive with every word.

SubhanAllah! This was nothing short of a miracle. Sulaiman praised Allah for all that he had learned and expressed his gratitude for the blessing of having Samaa return home safely. He then said a prayer for Shifaa, and for Nurah, and Hakeem, whose friendship was invaluable and whose support was always made available. Sulaiman rejoiced in that moment for all the good that had come from what he feared was a permanent blemish on his legacy. He forgave Nurah without any hesitation. She was his sister now—his sister in Islam, and he loved her as such.

That night, in Sulaiman's dream, the couple shared a most amazing adventure. It was a dream in which Sulaiman could fly and he took Samaa everywhere. They discovered places that neither of them had ever seen … magical places. Yet this wasn't magic. The universe was their freeway and they hurtled back and forth, among the stars, without restriction. Samaa gazed affectionately at this beautiful man escorting her across the midnight sky. She was starstruck. He had always been her hero, but tonight he was something more. They laughed and played together, encountering phenomena new and old, with each event more breathtaking than the last.

There was no difference in their physical creation here. They were neither human nor jinni but something different entirely. Whatever it was, they were the same in every way—except that Sulaiman could fly. He was stronger than ever, and yet he had never been more gentle. His voice was soothing, but he didn't need to use it. If he merely thought of an idea, Samaa instantly understood him, and vice versa. It was as if there were one soul between them. Just when she thought that nothing could be better than this, seven angels descended from the clouds and circled them as they hovered suspended in time and space.

A singular ray of light shone upon them, causing them to shimmer like the stars in the night sky above. Sulaiman reached for his wife and wrapped her in a loving embrace, as they began a slow descent toward the earth. Immediately, the first two angels spread their wings across the sky and dipped the tips into the well of Zamzam. They approached the entwined couple, one angel focusing on Sulaiman while the other tended to Samaa. Then, with a mighty flutter of their illustrious wings, droplets of the holy water sprinkled upon the faces and frames of the dreamer and his wife—purifying them from head to toe.

No sooner had the first pair retreated, than a second pair of angels descended upon the couple, again with an angel on either side, tending to them individually. These angels briefly separated the couple, shielding each spouse in a protective barrier of privacy within its wings. Sulaiman and Samaa were then clothed in purified, sacred garments and suspended, like ornaments, in the atmosphere.

The fifth heavenly being then burst across the sky into the eastern horizon, causing a jet stream the length of the entire earth. He ascended to the loftiest cloud and unraveled its properties into a delicate spool of ribbon. As he returned to Sulaiman and Samaa, he carefully united them once more, wrapping them in a perfect embrace with the miraculous ribbon made from the highest cloud in the sky.

When the sixth angel descended upon the couple, he exhaled a breath that left each of them mesmerized. Their eyes closed and their minds were taken to a place in the continuum of awareness between slumber and semiconsciousness. He cradled the union in his wing and delicately returned them to their bedroom. With that, the six angels descended in a perfect circle surrounding the blessed home, as they lifted their attention to the seventh and greatest angel among them.

He smiled with a face that shone like the moon but with greater brilliance. Then he extended his wings across the cosmos—eight pairs. A set of wings would flap and flutter, followed by another, in an extraordinary display of grandeur. Then he looked at the six angels who preceded him as they looked back at him. He raised his hands toward the heavens and bowed his head as the others followed suit. He praised Allah, glorifying His infinite Might and Majesty. Then a voice came from within him, carrying the names of Sulaiman and Samaa—two servants of Allah who demonstrated undying love for their Lord and for one another. The angel called upon the Lord to cover them in His Mercy and pour upon them unlimited blessings. His voice ascended into the heavens toward the Throne of Allah—where no righteous prayer can go unanswered. He concluded his supplication with the endorsement "Ameen," which was echoed by the six surrounding the home. Then he lowered his hands, and with a thunderous "whoosh," he forced the air beneath his wings and blasted off into the firmament. One by one the others whisked away in a similar fashion.

The next morning, Sulaiman arose before the alarm for Fajr and was surprised to find his darling still asleep. This was a rare opportunity for him to admire her in the peacefulness of rest, the way she often enjoyed watching him. He gazed upon her with vision that had adapted over the years, allowing his eyes to see her exactly as she appeared in his dreams. She was everything he had hoped for—both beautiful and loving— and as he lingered, his memory relived the incredible dream they had shared the previous night.

He decided not to wake her and instead began his morning worship with meditation and supplication. Several minutes later, she still hadn't budged. So he leaned over the bed to wake her with a kiss on her forehead. Slowly, she began to stir, and a delightful smile covered her face as she opened her eyes to the love of her life smiling back at her. She was unusually tired this morning and found it difficult to drag herself out of bed. Still, it was time for prayer, and Sulaiman was waiting to pray with her. Afterwards, they exchanged pleasantries in a warm embrace and reminisced on the dream before heading downstairs for breakfast and coffee. A busy workweek was ahead, and Sulaiman would be leaving earlier than normal to get in front of it.

Samaa was hammered by fatigue and couldn't shake free of it. She quickly straightened the kitchen after breakfast and returned to the bedroom to relax while listening to a recording of the Quran being recited. The beautiful recitation lulled her back to sleep, and when she opened her eyes again, she could hear Sulaiman's keys in the door as he came in from work. At this point, she began to worry. Something must be wrong with her. She had never slept a whole day in her entire life. While the trip to Indonesia was taxing, the inordinate amount of sleep didn't seem proportionate. Then it occurred to her that she might be jet lagged. Perhaps. It was an explanation that seemed to fit, but something about her condition made her uneasy—something she couldn't put her finger on.

Sulaiman kicked his shoes off and relaxed downstairs, mulling over another productive day at work. Samaa came down to greet him and sat next to him, leaning her head against his shoulder with her feet wrapped around his. He sometimes watched sports to decompress from a long day. So she handed him the remote and inquired, "How was work, love? Did you get a lot done?"

"Alhamdulillah, it was a good day. I like these guys, and I love their mission, but the contract is only for a week. That's not enough time to make an impact. I mean, I get it. They're a nonprofit on a tight budget, but—hey, wait a minute—are you just waking up?"

"Yeah, I don't know what's wrong with me. I'm exhausted. I slept all day."

"Seriously? Wow. Are you feeling alright?"

"Yeah, other than being worn out, I feel fine."

"Is it the trip? Jet lag maybe?"

"I don't know. I was thinking about that, but I've never known of jinn having jet lag."

"Yeah, babe, but come on, there are lots of things that apply to you that don't apply to most jinn. It's probably just your body getting back on track. Why? Are you feeling like it's something serious?"

"No. I'm not sick or anything like that. Maybe you're right. I guess it is the trip. I just know I feel like a sack of potatoes. Anyway … what were you saying?"

"Ohhh, babe … guess what? I forgot to tell you—"

"What?"

"Nejimah's pregnant!"

"Really? Masha'Allah, that's wonderful news."

"Yeah, she was beaming—smiling from ear to ear. I checked in on her and Bilal this weekend while you were in Indonesia. We had an awesome visit. Alhamdulillah, they seem to be doing really well."

"Alhamdulillah. I'm so happy for them. May Allah bless their family and give them the best. Ameen."

"Ameen. OK. So … I had an accident on the way home today."

"What! Why do you do that?"

"Do what?"

"Why do you wait and tell me the most important news last—and then you make it sound like a casual trip to the library."

"Babe, it was a minor fender bender … really. It was not that serious."

"OK. So if that's the case, why do you intentionally wait and tell me those things last? You do that all the time. That should have been the very first thing out of your mouth when you walked in."

"But love, you were upstairs when I walked in."

"Stop it. Stop it."

Sulaiman chuckled as he leaned over and kissed her cheek, calling for a truce. He knew she was right, but he never liked for her to worry. So he typically minimized the emphasis on negative incidents. This time, however, Samaa wasn't done with the conversation.

"Sulaiman, I worry about you just like you worry about me, and you're not protecting me when you withhold information. If something's wrong with you, I want to know. And I deserve to know. You're my best friend … my family. So what happened with the accident?"

"You're right, babe. I'm sorry. So it was a cab driver. I was coming around the frontage road by the airport, where the traffic funnels from the west terminal, and I was stopped at the traffic light. The girl next to me was on her phone not paying attention and didn't see the light change. These kids nowadays spend their entire lives on their iPhones. Anyway, the cab comes speeding off the interstate onto the frontage road behind the girl. He saw the light change, but she didn't; he anticipated that she would start going, but she didn't. By the time he reacted, he was too close to hit the breaks. So he veered out of her lane and into mine, clipping the back corner of my bumper—nothing major at all. But the real issue came when we got out to exchange insurance information."

"Oh why, what happened?"

"There were three passengers in the back of the taxi who were irate. Apparently, their flight was late—which made them late for a meeting. Then the accident made things worse. So they were rushing him the entire time and pressuring him not to wait for the police. As we're exchanging information, one guy gets out and starts screaming at us to hurry up—and sneezes all over us. They literally got into a fist fight right there—just plum ignorant. I didn't have time for that. So I went back to the car and waited for the police."

"So what did the police say?"

"Nothing, really. Everything had calmed down by then. They filed a report and gave him a ticket. That was it."

Samaa was pleased with him for sharing the details with her, and even happier that it was only a minor accident and he was safe. However, what neither of them realized was the overarching impact this day would ultimately have on the rest of their lives.

CHAPTER FIFTEEN

The symptoms of jet lag gradually began to subside as Samaa reacclimated with her normal routine. With each passing day, she felt more energetic, and by the weekend she was feeling like herself again. On Saturday, they attended Sulaiman's class at the masjid; afterwards, Samaa had a taste for ice cream. So they grabbed a quart on the way home. A quiet, relaxing evening was the perfect way to close out the week.

Sunday morning, Sulaiman woke up feeling achy, with a sore throat and light cough. Samaa was still sleeping—again. Every day since returning from Indonesia, she slept longer and later than ever before. Even though she stated that she was feeling better, the dramatic change in her sleeping pattern remained. Sulaiman was beginning to worry that something was wrong. He didn't want to wake her this morning, so he prayed alone and went down for coffee.

The sunrise was breathtaking as it peeked above the treetops—inviting him to bring his coffee to the back yard.

He nestled into the patio furniture and enjoyed his macchiato while studying from the Quran. Mornings like this imbued a wonderful sense of serenity: to be in solitude with nature, communing with Allah. His heart skipped along with the melody of his voice as he recited from the miraculous verses. After awhile, he noticed Samaa hadn't come down yet. So he went up to check on her. She was just beginning to awaken but wasn't feeling well. Her fatigue had returned and she was also battling nausea. Sulaiman spent the morning by her side, catering to his wife as she had always cared for him.

He pulled a rocking chair beside the bed and placed a glass of water on the nightstand. He sipped from the glass, allowing a droplet of water to slide onto his lower lip. Then he leaned over to Samaa and she drank it. There was nothing unusual about her consuming food or drink from her husband's lips—the amount of nourishment she required was minuscule in proportion to humans. A few droplets was more than enough to quench her thirst, and having him next to her made the pain more bearable. She could also tell that he wasn't feeling well either. He repeatedly cleared his throat, and though he tried to suppress his cough, a few got away from him. "What's wrong, love?" she asked.

"Nothing. Just a cold. I'll be fine." In this moment, Samaa was his only concern. Besides, Sulaiman felt that with a heavy dose of lemon and honey, he'd be as good as new within a day or two. His wife, on the other hand, clearly had something going on.

Monday morning, Samaa seemed fully recovered as Sulaiman continued to battle flu-like symptoms. He shrugged it off and went to work as he normally would—with lemon and honey in tow. He had two important meetings that he couldn't afford to miss; the flu would simply have to take a back seat to higher priorities. However, by early afternoon, it was clear that his symptoms were winning the battle. Sulaiman was forced to leave work to tend to his illness. He spent the next two days working from home and supplemented his lemon and honey regimen with over-the-counter medications. Even so, his condition grew significantly worse. By Thursday afternoon, Samaa insisted he seek medical attention. So they made an appointment for early the next morning to give him enough time to attend Jumuah prayer afterwards.

As they lay in bed that night, Sulaiman sniffled and sneezed, tossing and turning with the pillow, as he tried to find a comfortable sleeping position. He finally settled with his back turned to Samaa. She scooted close, snuggling behind him, with her arm draped across his shivering body. She eventually rolled away and fell into a deep sleep.

Suddenly, in the middle of the night, her eyes opened. The bedroom ceiling was painted with every star in the sky—until she realized she wasn't looking at the ceiling. Confused, Samaa rubbed her eyes as she struggled to gather her bearings. This was a dream ... but Sulaiman's dreams weren't usually so abrupt. They never caught her off guard like this. As the scene unfolded, she lay still, waiting for her husband's subconscious to appear. The alluring night sky was as beautiful as she remembered, and as she waited for Sulaiman, the same seven angels from the previous dream descended from the heavens and summoned her.

Her being lifted from the bed and began to levitate beyond her control—another event that was not characteristic of Sulaiman's dreams. Nervous energy bubbled inside as she ascended into the sky above her bedroom. The cool night air caressed her cheeks and helped to settle her nerves a bit, but there was still no sign of Sulaiman. Then she turned to look back and discovered him lying peacefully undisturbed in their bed. Instantly, panic set in—panic and the reality that this was not Sulaiman's dream. This time, Samaa was alone.

Every emotion raced inside of her, and as her temperature climbed, the colors on the surface of her being were altered. The translucent rainbows that normally danced in her eyes had scattered, and what remained was solid indigo. Her face was violet, her lips blue. The green had run to her fingers and toes and her core was blazing red. She was terrified. The only action she could think to take was to close her eyes and pray. She called upon Allah in desperation, fearing that this was the moment of her death or the onset of the Day of Judgment.

As she rose into the sky, the angels formed a circle around her. All but one hovered with wings fully extended across the firmament, some extending beyond the solar system, others beyond the Milky Way and deep into the extremities of the universe. The majestic display was awe-inspiring, but Samaa missed most of it with closed eyes. When she was finally comfortable enough to open them, she found the angels smiling at her—all but one.

The seventh and greatest of the angels remained calm, subdued even, wrapped in the cover of all eight pairs of his wings. Then two by two, each pair of wings began to flap and flutter in an extravagant display more beautiful than before— ultimately revealing a child that he cradled in his arms. It was the most beautiful soul Samaa had ever seen—delicate and pristine. The angel approached. Then as Samaa collected her arms in the shape of a cradle, the soul of the child was placed in her embrace. She was instantly and completely filled with love, and as she feasted her eyes on the miracle child in her arms, the rainbows in her complexion were fully restored.

Next, the angel extended his wing down into the bedroom and plucked something from Sulaiman as he rested. Gracefully, the wing returned to the child and gently placed inside it whatever had been taken from Sulaiman. The angel smiled at Samaa and her soul was enveloped in tranquility. Finally, the congregation said a prayer on behalf of Samaa and her family, as they ascended beyond the stars and out of sight. Simultaneously, the soul of the child disappeared as it was absorbed into the core of Samaa's being.

In the blink of an eye, she was back in bed, opening her eyes to the tickle of a soft wind being blown in her face by her loving husband. She smiled through squinting eyes and stretched her arms wide before wrapping them around his neck and declaring her love for him. What an incredible morning this was. For the first time in her life, she was awakened from a dream that did not exist in the subconscious of Sulaiman. Allah had gifted Samaa with her own dream—a dream that blessed her with joy beyond measure.

During the morning drive to the doctor's office, she pondered over the dream's interpretation. Could it be that this was a true dream, or was the child a metaphor for something else? She was itching to share her thoughts with Sulaiman, but now didn't seem like the appropriate time. He had his doctor's appointment and then Jumuah prayer immediately after. Besides, this was exciting for her and she wanted him to be in better spirits when she shared the news. So she waited.

Unfortunately, what they learned from the doctor would delay the topic a bit longer. Sulaiman had contracted a unique strand of the most recent iteration of coronavirus. He was immediately sent home to quarantine.

Sulaiman's condition worsened over the next couple of days, but Samaa stayed with him as he fought to return to full health. It worked in their favor that she was not susceptible to human disease. Having to quarantine was already bad enough, but to do so apart from his wife would be considerably worse. She remained by his side, sometimes as coach, other times as cheerleader, ensuring that he never tired in his fight. His tolerance for pain allowed him to ignore the body aches after awhile, but the labored breathing was becoming more of a challenge. Their main objective was to practice strategies to curb the symptoms long enough for the virus to run its course. Daily, Sulaiman reminded himself that patience means perseverance, and in every moment of this trial he remained firm, never doubting the Mercy of Allah.

Then one morning, he finally seemed to be improving. His cough was nearly nonexistent and the body aches had all but dissipated. He felt healthy and energized, eager to go outside. He ate a full breakfast for the first time in more than a week. Then he headed into the backyard for fresh air and exercise. Samaa floated off the ground with excitement. She could see a renewed bounce in his step, and she playfully swirled around him as he walked with bare feet across the grass. They laughed and stared into one another's eyes, realizing what a gift this moment was. The weather was amazing. Their chemistry was incredible. This was her moment—the perfect opportunity to share her dream with him.

As Samaa narrated the dream, Sulaiman listened intently, captivated by the imagery she described. There was no doubt in his mind that this was a true dream, announcing to Samaa that they would soon be blessed with a beautiful child. When they went back inside, Sulaiman noticed a missed call on the screen of his phone. It was from Nejimah, so he immediately called back.

"As Salaamu alaikum, Daddy"

"Wa alaikum salaam, my princess."

"How are you feeling today?"

"Much better, Alhamdulillah. How are you?"

The sound of her dad's voice was always comforting, and today, it was especially nice to hear the extra bit of oomph in his tone. Nejimah was having a tough time with her dad's illness but didn't want to let on that she was worried. He was the strongest man she'd ever known, and in her eyes, he could withstand anything. However, there was something she wasn't sharing—something that burdened her heavily.

"What's wrong Nej, is everything OK? You seem distracted."

"Huh? … Oh … yeah, sorry Dad. I'm fine. Just tired and loopy I guess."

"You sure? How's the baby?"

"Alhamdulillah, the baby's really good. We had a checkup the other day."

"And Bilal?"

"He's good."

"Oh. OK. Well, did you need something earlier? I'm sorry I missed you. I was outside in the backyard."

"Oh … no. Just checking in to see how you're doing."

"OK, well I won't hold you, princess. Talk to you later—"

"Hey, Daddy!"

"Yeah, sweetie."

"Do you remember when we went to pick roses in the flower garden up in the hills?"

"Of course. How could I ever forget? It was after I sent your first bouquet of roses to your school. Mommy said you were so excited when she picked you up that day—said you were dancing in the clouds. Then we had to go pick more the next week because you didn't realize that flowers die after a few days."

"That's one of my favorite memories, Daddy. Picking flowers in the garden with you was one of the best days of my life."

"Mine too, baby."

Then, with a crackle in her voice and a tear dripping from the corner of her eye, she whispered, "I'm not ready for this, Daddy. I'm not ready yet."

"Oh Nejimah, you're going to make a wonderful mother, princess."

"No. Not that, Dad. I'm not ready to lose you. I'm worried about you."

"Aw Nej, you know me. I'm in great shape. Besides, I'm too stubborn to let a cough take me out. I'll be back out there in no time, insha-Allah. Talk to me, sweetie. What's wrong?"

What Nejimah was reluctant to share was that she'd had a bad dream. One that jolted her from her sleep and had plagued her thoughts ever since. It occurred the night Sulaiman last came to visit, and until now, she hadn't shared the dream with anyone. Her father always taught her not to describe bad dreams but to pray about them instead. This time, however, she needed to share.

In the dream, she saw her dad holding the first bouquet of roses he'd ever sent to her. He was as handsome as ever, smiling at his beloved princess. That smile ... it was everything to a daughter who relished it—like sunshine in the spring. It was the symbol of a father's love who never disapproved of her and cherished her more than life itself. The roses were more radiant than any she'd ever seen—though it was clear they were the same roses from her childhood. This was a most delightful dream ... until it wasn't.

The flowers began to fade, as did the light in her father's eyes, and the rich color in his skin. The green stems turned black as rose petals began to wilt and decay. Sulaiman's hands began to wrinkle, his legs bowed, his face began to wither and his eyes closed. Still, his beautiful smile never dimmed. He was lowered into a grave and briefly out of sight. When she saw him again, he lay motionless, at peace with his arms crossed atop his chest—still holding on to her roses. Then there was a twinkle of light, and each of her roses bloomed with renewed radiance. Nejimah gasped with anticipation, focusing on her dad to see what would happen next, only to find her dream interrupted by a heart too anxious to know the ending.

In an attempt to console her, Sulaiman explained to Nejimah what she already knew: only Allah could know the true meaning of her dream. It didn't necessarily mean that

Sulaiman would succumb to his illness. He insisted that his health was improving and today was his best day in a long while. Nonetheless, he understood his daughter's concern. So they prayed together—asking Allah for the best possible outcome.

Later, Sulaiman found himself standing in front of the mirror, contemplating the particulars of a most peculiar day. He was struck by the profound balance in creation. Namely that all things are created in pairs: male and female, night and day, life and death. Moreover, this day had pointed out the inescapable reality that life, in all its ups and downs, never truly falls out of balance—not on the scale of Allah. For in perfect symmetry, a pair of dreams had come bearing two halves of a singular message—that life and death are inextricably tied and each are in the sole possession of Allah. The announcement had come via the two most important individuals in Sulaiman's life—a life which was perhaps in its final chapter.

Staring into the eyes of his own reflection, he reckoned with himself: *Ya Sulaiman, have you enjoyed the favors of your Lord? Did you find His Mercy lacking or His Command unjust? Of course not. So consider what you owe ... in what condition are you returning what you were entrusted with? Are you ready for this meeting that you have always known to be certain? How will you be assessed? In your own estimation, have you fulfilled every obligation befitting His Majesty—or have you fallen short? What have you earned in the final verdict, man? Oh son of*

Adam, you have a choice. Do not choose to die in a state other than total submission to your Creator.

He would spend the entire night in prayer, falling asleep on his prayer rug in the early hours of the morning.

CHAPTER SIXTEEN

uarantine restrictions mandated that Sulaiman spend the next two days at home alone, while Samaa traveled with her aunt and uncle to a pregnancy specialist. Aurora was a longtime friend of Sakina's, and she was an expert in abnormal pregnancy and childbirth among jinn. Without any hesitation, she confirmed that Samaa was pregnant. She further explained that procreation between humans and jinn is extremely rare, and thus there isn't a set of established norms with regard to expectations. Samaa would need to listen carefully to her own biology and be ready to react accordingly. Her symptoms were likely to be intermittent rather than constant and would probably not be relegated to one particular trimester or time frame. In general, jinn experience different symptoms than human mothers, but Aurora expected that Samaa would likely experience both types of symptoms at different stages in her pregnancy.

Upon returning home, Samaa was surprised to find her husband collapsed on the bedroom floor. He lay covered in sweat, barely conscious and gasping for air. He reeked of the vomit soiling the carpet beneath his face. Yet he refused to surrender. His limbs quivered profusely, trying to lift his body upright—though the effort would not avail him. Samaa rushed to his side, wiping his face and helping him turn to his back. Next, she would move him into a sitting position, but not before taking a few moments' rest. Sulaiman was extremely heavy to maneuver. His energy was depleted and he was too weak to provide any substantial leverage. For the first time in years, Samaa considered possessing his body to help him stand up. She didn't do it, but she thought about it. Eventually, her perseverance paid off and Sulaiman was in a stable sitting position that allowed him to finally catch his breath.

If there was ever a devoted wife to her husband, Samaa Sanders was it. By nightfall, Sulaiman was notably better because Samaa had forced him to eat and helped him bathe before getting him settled into bed. Now, as he relaxed beside her, he was comforted by the soothing sound of her voice. She talked to him about everything and nothing—just spending quality time with him. When she told him about her visit with Aurora, he smiled. He had already known. His heart provided all the confirmation he needed. He placed his fingertips upon his lips and kissed them. Then he reached over and placed his fingers over Samaa's core (where his baby was nestled inside of her) and kissed the baby with his fingertips. He was careful not to overexert himself after all she had done to get him comfortably positioned.

As the couple held hands, Sulaiman asked if she would hover above him, so he could look into her eyes. There was something he wanted to tell her. It had been awhile since she'd done that, and when she did, it brought back old memories. Sulaiman shared the details of Nejimah's dream and confessed, "My love, I don't think I will recover from this illness … but Allah knows best."

She offered an endearing smile and kissed his forehead, saying, "Don't worry, my love. I believe you will recover fully, and that is easy for Allah to accomplish. But if He decides to bring you nearer to Himself, then certainly your Lord is better company for you than we are." This made Sulaiman smile. He was impressed by her response and filled with gratitude for this incredible gift from Allah: his wife. Samaa had been an extraordinary partner, and together they had shared an extraordinary life.

After tucking Sulaiman in, Samaa stepped away to gather herself. She wanted her teammate to see that her faith would not be shaken by this ordeal. She did not, however, want him to see the depth of her pain at the thought of living without him. In the guest bedroom, farthest away from where her husband slept, Samaa sat in the closet processing her emotions. She knew that life must come to an end, but she wanted a little more time. Sulaiman was strong and she knew he could make it through this; but nothing is possible without Allah. So she pleaded with the Lord: "Please Allah, don't take him away from us yet. Who will our child be without his father? I want him to know the man I married … the man You created to make my world a better place. I found Islam through him and I found my happiness with him. I don't want to be selfish, but let him stay with me for a while longer and allow him to meet our child. "

She cried herself to sleep.

The next morning, Samaa pressed speed the dial on Sulaiman's phone for Nejimah. After the first ring, Nejimah answered, only to be greeted by silence. She waited awhile, "Hello? … Daddy?" There was no answer, so she hung up. The phone rang again, and again there was silence. Samaa was speaking, but Nejimah couldn't hear her. Again, she hung up the phone. Samaa persisted, calling over and over until Nejimah was forced to get in the car and come over.

Feeling uneasy, Nejimah walked into her garage, flicked the light on, and tried remembering where she stored the gym bag. She remembered—in the stackable totes. She slung the bag into the back seat and exited the garage down the driveway. The entire drive to The Meadows was a blur, but somehow she was parked in front of the home she'd known her whole life. She sat there terrified—afraid of the news that her father had died, and equally afraid of entering a contaminated home with her unborn child.

Formulating a plan of approach, she unzipped the gym bag and pulled a Level B hazmat suit from it. Incredulously, she unfolded it, trying to wrap her head around what was happening. Obviously, it was Samaa calling from her dad's phone—which would indicate bad news. So she braced for the worst.

The beat of her heart was audible inside her head as she walked in slow motion around the side of the house and into the backyard. She stopped and waited at the kitchen door … not for anything in particular … just waited. She sucked the deepest possible breath into her nostrils and slowly eased it out through puckered lips—savoring the oxygen inside her. Then before she could take another step, she frantically shook her hands, as if they were wet with nervousness, and wrung them dry inside one another before putting on gloves. Finally, she tapped on the kitchen door.

Eerily, the handle twisted and the door opened with Samaa standing at the threshold—invisible and inaudible to Nejimah. However, in this critical moment that would need to change. There were no two individuals on earth closer to Sulaiman than his wife and daughter, and for him, they would need to find a way to communicate. Nejimah knew Samaa was standing there. So she greeted her, not realizing that Samaa had been speaking since the door first opened. By now, she was all but screaming, and Nejimah still couldn't hear her. The two were at an impasse with no indication of how to move forward.

Nejimah closed her eyes and quieted her mind, asking Allah to intervene. In similar fashion, Samaa petitioned,

"Lord, please show me what to do." Then as Nejimah focused her concentration, Samaa floated beside her. She placed her lips beneath the fabric of the hazmat suit—until they were touching Nejimah's ear. She channeled her love for Sulaiman, allowing it to be the vehicle for the words she chose next.

"As Salaamu alaikum, precious daughter of Sulaiman. It is an honor to finally meet you after learning so much about you from your father. May Allah reward you for the kindness you've shown him; I am a witness that you are the twinkle in his eye and the great love of his life. Thank you for coming. I thought it was important to have you here with us today."

Nejimah squinted her eyes, listening intently to the faint voice inside her ear. The moment couldn't be more surreal. Although she knew her father would never lie about his unconventional marriage, the reality of Samaa was something Nejimah had allowed herself to file away in the back of her mind. So hearing Samaa's voice for the first time conjured emotions Nejimah didn't realize were there.

Samaa explained that Sulaiman's condition had worsened and she wanted him to enjoy his daughter's company to lift his spirits. They discussed a plan to minimize the risk for Nejimah—who continued waiting outside while Samaa prepared the home and retrieved Sulaiman. When she entered the bedroom, he was resting. So she woke him with a light prodding, "Love, I'm sorry to wake you but I need you downstairs. Nejimah is here and she wants to see you. Come on, dear, Bismillah."

Sulaiman was barely coherent, but with Samaa's constant coaching—and the desire to see his daughter—he slowly made his way downstairs and onto the sofa. Moments later, Nejimah entered through the kitchen and into the living room, where she saw her dad yawning as he sat up on fluffed pillows. Their eyes met, and she almost broke down but managed to keep it together. He was such a proud man. Even now he wanted to be a pillar of strength for his daughter. So he sat up straight and attempted to disguise any weakness or discomfort. She didn't need him to do that though. She would love her father until he couldn't move a muscle; and in her eyes, he would always be Superman.

When Sulaiman coughed, his entire body shook. He spoke in a raspy voice with labored breathing; it wouldn't be much longer before a ventilator would be unavoidable. Nejimah hugged her dad before taking a seat next to him and sharing, "It's really good to see you, Daddy. I was missing you."

"I was missing you too, sweet pea, and I'm always happy to see your face."

"Even with this silly mask on?"

"Alhamdulillah, I praise Allah for every opportunity to see you, in any way that I can. I never get tired of my princess. But what are doing here, Nej? You shouldn't be here. You have the baby to consider."

"I know Daddy, but look at me—I'm Fort Knox. Insha-Allah, we'll be fine."

179

"You know what I think? I think you're having a boy. I can feel it. He's gonna be something special, Nej. I can't wait to meet him. Oh yeah, I didn't get a chance to tell you yet, but Samaa is pregnant too."

"Oh wow, really? SubhanAllah, that's amazing."

"Yeah, Alhamdulillah, we're excited. I'm pretty sure it's a girl. Allah knows best, but I think you have a little sister on the way."

Nejimah placed her father's hand between the two of hers and held it tightly. She wished she could lean her cheek against it, the way she'd always done when she was sad or troubled. Unfortunately, today, the necessary barriers would not afford that option. Still, she was happy to be with him—to be looking directly into his eyes and not at a memory in her mind. This moment was real—an opportunity to touch him and be near him in person, in the home she grew up in. Her father was everything to her, and in the waning moments of his life, being in his presence was priceless.

She put her arms around him, holding him as he hacked and coughed. None of that mattered. What mattered was that they were together as they had always been. She accepted that she might not ever have a chance to see him again after today, or feel his gentle kiss on her forehead. Somehow, Allah would help her find a way to handle it; but for now, she savored every single second with the first man who had ever loved her. As a Muslim and expecting mother, Nejimah felt ready, but as a daughter, the prospect of facing the world without either of her parents made her feel lost.

Allah will not place a burden upon any shoulder heavier than it can bear. This much she knew. It's what her father had always taught, and how they both made it through the tragedy of her mother's death. But this felt different. When her mother died, Nejimah could feel how much her dad still loved her mom. She could see it in the way he mourned and hear it in his voice when he reminisced. It made her mother seem less dead because she lived on in her father's love. But if he was dying now, then her mother was dying all over again and taking him with her this time.

The little girl inside Nejimah's heart was as terrified as she'd ever been, afraid of doing this all alone. Yes, her husband was as supportive a man as she could hope to find, but her relationship with her dad was lifelong. He knew her before she knew herself and his love shaped her existence. He saw her first steps, first tooth, first bike, high school graduation, and he was the only one to dry her tears and ease the pain of losing her mother.

The hour was getting late, but Nejimah wasn't ready to leave. She held on to her father for as long as she could, reminding him of stories that he'd forgotten and listening to him do the same. Even in sickness, his mind was sharp. He knew she was holding on to this moment and afraid to leave—that she equated leaving with letting go. Sulaiman turned to face his daughter. He looked her in the eye with an expression that assured her that everything would be OK and asked, "Do you know that I love you?"

"Yes, of course."

"And do you know that Allah loves you, and His Mercy extends beyond the heavens and the earth?"

"Yes, sir."

"Nejimah, I'm proud of you. You are everything I could have hoped for, and I'm pleased with you in every way. There's no need to fear—none whatsoever. One thing is certain to me and I hope is certain to you: I will die before my love for you ever does. Even if I were to make a full recovery tomorrow morning, that would not negate the certainty of my death. Death is certain, sweetie. These are the lessons we learn over and over. But what I want you to know is that if my death should come in two days or twenty years, my love for you will live far beyond that. So focus on that, my precious. Focus on that. Don't worry about this sickness. Go home and see about Bilal. Say your prayers and get some rest. Don't let one moment in time stop you from living. Even if this is my last breath, don't let your life stop here. The best way to honor me is to keep living out this beautiful life that I have dreamed for you. Whatever is coming will come; but now it's time for rest. I love you with all of my heart, and that has always been enough between me and you. So take my love with you ... tonight and always."

He kissed her gloved hands and shooed his daughter away.

CHAPTER SEVENTEEN

The sun came up and peeked through the blinds in her bedroom window. Nejimah squinted her eyes and stretched, as she imagined the sound of her mother's voice saying, "Stretch … and reach the stars." The pillow beneath her remained damp from weary eyes flooded with tears. Morning had come too quickly. Realizing she had overslept, Nejimah forced herself out of bed to go pray.

As she continued with her morning routine, she purposely avoided her phone, fearing bad news was on the horizon. She would eventually get around to returning calls, but in the short term, her coping strategy was "no news is good news." After a few hours passed, she wanted to check in with Bilal, who had left for work prior to her waking that morning. She still wasn't ready for any news concerning her dad. So she grabbed her phone and pressed the speed dial, looking away from the screen. Bilal answered, and just as he did, the doorbell rang. "Answer the door, honey," he suggested. To Nejimah's surprise, it was a bouquet of roses from her husband. Bilal knew she was stressed and had ordered the floral delivery to brighten her day. It was important to him that Nejimah understood she wasn't alone in her struggle. He would always be there for her—not because she was pregnant, or out of obligation, but because he was in love with her and was committed to her happiness. He had witnessed Nejimah's relationship with her father and knew exactly what was required to love this woman. From the very first moment they met, that had become his mission.

Nejimah signed for the bouquet and sniffed the roses. They were beautiful and smelled exactly like love. Bilal had taken a page from her father's book, and she loved him for that. The sound of his voice was a welcome distraction from her heavy heart; he knew the perfect balance of when to speak and when to listen. As the brief conversation came to a close, he blew a kiss through the phone and said goodbye. Almost instantly her sadness returned. It wasn't merely that she was losing her father. It was the timing. She was pregnant with her first child, and the heaviness of misfortune was cheating her out of the happiness of motherhood.

When Nejimah finally decided to look at her phone, she knew instantly that her worst fears had come to pass. There was an unintelligible text that most certainly had come from Samaa; it could only have one meaning. She didn't even bother with a response. In fact, she did nothing at all. She couldn't move. She just stood there, stranded in time and completely numb. There were no words to say, no tears to cry, just … nothing. Then, out of nowhere, it came to her—her father's voice inside her head, reminding her of everything he had said the night before. "*Don't allow one moment in time to stop your life.*" She held on to that thought—thereby holding on to her dad—and knew that somehow, some way, everything was going to be alright.

She didn't go over to the house that day. Her heart couldn't take it—not two days in a row. Instead, she contacted Aamir, a family friend who was the director of Islamic funeral services for all of Eagleton. She asked him to go by the house and check on her father.

Aamir pulled into the driveway and went to ring the doorbell. No one answered. After waiting several minutes, he grabbed his phone from the car and called Nejimah. She didn't answer either. Before leaving, he decided to try the doorbell one final time; when he went back, he found the door open. "As Salaamu alaikum," he announced as he cautiously entered the home. There was an unsealed envelope on the bottom step in the foyer, and he opened it to find Sulaiman's last will and testament. Before going any farther, he called the police.

Fifteen minutes later, a black and white cruiser pulled up and two officers got out. Aamir showed his credentials and explained the phone call he received from Nejimah. The officers inspected the premises and discovered Sulaiman's body lying peacefully in bed with his arms folded, as though he'd been praying. They examined Sulaiman's will and called for paramedics to come and take his body. When the ambulance pulled away, Aamir followed them to the hospital and waited for the medical examiner to complete protocol. Eventually, Sulaiman's remains were released in accordance with his wishes.

Meanwhile, Samaa informed her aunt and uncle that her husband had passed away. Sakina went back to the house with Samaa to keep her company. Hakeem, on the other hand, went to pay his respects to Sulaiman. He rounded up a few brothers to join him, and they dashed off to the funeral home. When they arrived, Aamir's assistants were removing Sulaiman from the vehicle. Some of the jinn rushed to help escort the body into the mortuary.

The walls inside were solemn with the stillness of death, showing respect for some, pity for others. This was not a place for light-heartedness. There was an inconspicuous sitting area adjacent to Aamir's office, near the entrance. Aside from that, every room in the small building was for the dead. They secured Sulaiman onto the stretcher and rolled him down a freezing cold hallway. The door at the end led to a washroom, where his body would be prepared for the grave. A short while later, Aamir entered the washroom with Bilal following closely behind.

Bilal was instructed to secure the head of his father-in-law, while the two assistants flanked either side of the table, holding a sheet over the body. This was to ensure that Sulaiman's dignity would always be maintained and his private areas would never go uncovered. As Aamir began washing the body, he felt a tickle on his arm and instructed the assistants to keep the sheet at an appropriate height. What he didn't realize was that the sheet never touched him. The tickle on his arm was because of Hakeem—who participated in washing Sulaiman alongside Aamir. Hakeem synchronized with Aamir, as they gently cared for the body of his longtime friend. Sulaiman was now on a journey to meet his Lord; and Hakeem wanted to personally be involved in fulfilling his last rights. This would be his final act of love for a man he held in the highest esteem. Sulaiman's Janazah service was held at the masjid the following day. Afterwards, he was taken to the Islamic cemetery where he was finally laid to rest.

* * * * *

Hakeem returned to the Sanders residence with what seemed a multitude of Muslim jinn. They had come from far and wide to attend the Janazah and burial. Upon entering the home, the sisters embraced Samaa, expressing their condolences. They found helpful ways to assist around the house so she could relax and take it easy. Hakeem gave the brothers a guided tour of the home, narrating stories of his niece's incredible marriage, which had now ascended to celebrity status.

Samaa was gracious and kept a smile on her face, though inside, she was immensely lonely. Her home was filled with guests, but they were all practically strangers, and though she appreciated the expressions love and thoughtfulness, it was overwhelming. It was the same conversation every five seconds with a different individual: "Thank you for coming … yes … Alhamdulillah … insha-Allah … ameen." She stood in her living room staring across a sea of faces, and not one reminded her of her beloved Sulaiman. Suddenly, she blinked and the world began to make sense again. Samaa squinted her eyes, thinking they were playing tricks, when the image of a hijab flashed behind a group of sisters who were talking in the foyer.

Investigating what she thought she'd seen, Samaa rushed toward the foyer. Then, to her delight, the heavenly face of Nurah emerged from the crowd. They clasped one another in an emotional embrace. Nurah had come all the way from Indonesia to pay her respects and be with her friend. Her eyes perused the room and saw a life she thought she'd left behind forever. This home represented the worst part of her existence, and she had intensely debated whether or not to return. Ultimately, she decided that her duty to honor Sulaiman and support Samaa were more important than her reservations.

Having Nurah show up was an absolute blessing for Samaa. She was the only individual who truly understood what Samaa was going through—being intimately familiar with the home, the family, Sulaiman's character, and other dynamics too difficult to explain to someone else. Most of the brothers had already gone into the backyard. However, Nurah requested that Hakeem clear out the remaining stragglers. She then summoned the sisters into the living room for a brief discussion. There were so many guests that some sat cross-legged on the floor while others levitated in sitting positions above their heads.

Nurah sat on the sofa with Samaa and Sakina. She gently grabbed Samaa by the hand—interlacing their fingers—and addressed the guests:

"Sisters, on behalf of Sulaiman and Samaa, may Allah reward you for this outstanding display of support in your coming out today. The family is grateful beyond words, but now it's time to allow them the opportunity to process their emotions in dealing with their loss. I know that many of you have come to show solidarity and to honor the memory of one of the few human beings given access into our world. I'm also aware that curiosity plays a factor as well. So allow me to share a few words about this remarkable individual whom Samaa had the great fortune to call her husband."

Nurah poured accolades upon the memory of her former foe, confirming to the audience that he was as good a man as all the rumors described—even better. She told stories that reminded Samaa of falling in love with the man of her dreams, and all that they shared together. Samaa closed her eyes and leaned her head against Nurah's shoulder. Then a room full of wide-eyed jinn looked on in amazement as real tears poured from her eyes.

A week later, Nejimah came by the house for the first time since her father passed away. She and Bilal had welcomed into their home numerous guests who expressed their condolences for the loss of her father. Yet none of that was as emotional as entering the house where her heart could still feel her father's presence. It was time to start the process of tying up loose ends; she was also concerned about Samaa and wanted to check on her. The first thing she noticed upon walking in was how spotless the house remained. Samaa had kept everything in order, as if Sulaiman were still alive. Nejimah closed the door behind her and Samaa instantly felt her presence. A breath of fresh air surged through the home and completely uplifted its energy. Samaa leapt from the bed and rushed to the top of the stairs. It was so good to see her. Seeing the face of his daughter brought her husband back home, if only for a second.

Nejimah called out, announcing her arrival and wondering if Samaa was still in the home. Samaa responded in a voice too low to be heard, "Welcome home, Nejimah. Welcome back to your home. This house longs for your presence as I long to be with your father." Samaa followed her into the kitchen and watched as Nejimah opened the refrigerator—surprised to see it was adequately stocked. Not a single perishable was spoiled. She grabbed a bottled water and proceeded through the rest of the home with Samaa following closely behind.

This was not an empty house. Nejimah could feel the life inside It. It felt close ... warm ... familiar. She called out again: "Samaa, I'm not sure if you can hear me, but my heart tells me you can. Thank you for taking care of my dad. Thank you so much. It means the world to me that you gave me an opportunity to see him the night before he died. I'll never be able to repay you for that.

"It's funny, you know. I never understood your marriage because I never really tried, but for my own selfish reasons, I was happy with it. My father being married to a jinni was easier to accept than if he had married another human. It was easier because you were easier for me to ignore.

"But now I realize how flawed that was. Daddy loved you, Samaa. And I feel like I let you both down. Insha-Allah, that will never happen again. In my heart, you are now and forever a part of our family. Even at this very moment, I can feel the love in this house ... and I know exactly what that feels like. Love—in this house—is more familiar to me than anything else in the world."

Inspired by the love in her heart, and a million happy memories, Nejimah dug up the old home movies and popped a bag of popcorn. Samaa sat on the sofa beside her as they both relived the happiest moments in their lives. This was the beginning of a bond that would grow far beyond either of their expectations.

CHAPTER EIGHTEEN

The sound of thunder tore through the clouds and crashed into the house as if the sky was literally breaking. Nejimah's eyes popped open to the quiver of her heart and the pitter patter of a downpour drumming at the window. That was how it started. She massaged the dull pain in her belly hoping to quickly return to sleep. Half an hour later, she was still massaging with a grimace on her face—inhaling hisses through exposed teeth. An hour after that, the worsening pain lifted her from the bed and curled her to her knees, with no other choice but to wake Bilal.

With all the nerves of a first-time father on the night of his child's birth, Bilal jumped to his wife's aid. He had the passionate devotion of a knight in shining armor and the coordination of a dancer with two left feet. He was so anxious, they had to practice Nejimah's delivery breathing in order to calm his nerves. He repeatedly reminded himself that tonight he was assigned the easy job while his wife would do the heavy lifting. This helped to center his focus and keep him calm.

Nejimah wanted to deliver her baby in the home where she was raised. So they had consulted a midwife, and all the preparations were made to facilitate her wishes. Now that she was in labor, Bilal alerted the midwife that the time had come. He grabbed the birthing bag—which was prepared months in advance—and escorted his wife to the car. The drive took forever, as Nejimah sat writhing in pain with each contraction. Finally, they were parked in the driveway.

Bilal ran inside first and placed the birthing bag in the foyer, with a small carry-on suitcase. He then rushed back for his wife and walked with her as she waddled to the door, with one arm on her belly and the other around his neck. He was part support, part victim, as the unrelenting choke hold left him impressed with his wife's newly acquired strength. Upon entering, Nejimah was immediately struck by the sound of a blood-curdling scream. It was Samaa—whose voice was as clear and resonant as any human's—announcing that she was in labor too.

By Allah's destiny, the births of Sulaiman's youngest child and first grandchild were synchronized. On the seventh day of the week, in the seventh month of the year, at 7:07 in the morning, the two children simultaneously emerged and were welcomed into the home at 7707 Sprite Meadow Court. They announced their presence to the world by glorifying the Lord with screams at the top of their tiny little voices.

Nejimah gazed adoringly at her beautiful little boy—the son her father predicted. Unsurprisingly, they chose to name him Sulaiman, and he was the instant cure for his mother's aching heart. As she stared into the curious eyes peeking back at her, she gained a better sense of the enormous love her parents felt for her. If only she could fulfill the role of parenthood as gracefully as they had demonstrated. That was her prayer. She longed for them and wished they could be with her in sharing this experience. Even so, she was immensely grateful, for her bundle of joy allowed no room for sadness.

Insisting that Nejimah take the master suite, Samaa moved into the guest bedroom in the far corner of the house. She could finally breathe a sigh of relief after a long night of what felt like torture. Yet, for the miraculous wonder she held in her arms, she would gladly endure it again—a million times over. The rainbows in her eyes danced like never before at the sight of the most stunningly beautiful soul, whom she would call Yusra. Sulaiman had accurately predicted the birth of his daughter, and he was also responsible for the selection of her name. It was the kiss on his fingertips the night he collapsed. When he placed his fingers on Samaa's core, he recited the verse "Fa inna ma'al usri yusra" (Certainly with difficulty comes ease).

Her husband's comforting reminder stayed with Samaa as she agonized in the death grip of childbirth. He was her only solace in the dire throes of anguish, his blessed image permanently imprinted in her memory. Even now, she could hear the sound of his voice reminding her that—for the believers—triumph will always follow tragedy, because Allah has promised to give us ease with every difficulty. Her daughter, Yusra, was exactly that.

Yusra was a happy baby from the very beginning. She cried for only twenty seconds before a smile graced her face and a vibrant chuckle burst from within her. She was a jinni by all appearances—except one. In the core of her being was an exact replica of her father's beating heart. In fact, it was a piece of his heart, removed by the angel the night she was given to her mother. There were no other signs of humanness within her—and even her heart would remain cloaked with invisibility until she grew older.

After a day of rest, the adoring mothers introduced one another to the newest members of their family. Nejimah could actually see her little sister more clearly than she saw Samaa—though the latter was becoming easier, the more time they spent together. The newborns were instantly drawn to one another—cooing and flailing their limbs involuntarily. Their innate connection, their familial ties, and the destiny of Allah would permanently bind them to one another, and they would forever be known, to men and jinn, as "the twins."

Soon, it became apparent that Yusra was growing more rapidly than her nephew, and as she grew, her humanness began to reveal itself. Physical human attributes would intermittently appear upon her and then disappear within a matter of hours. One morning she had eyes with pupils in them and eyelids that blinked. Another day her hands were made of flesh and produced fingerprints. Occasionally, she even produced human waste after eating. Samaa soon realized that her daughter would eventually resemble humans in every way. What she hadn't realized was that Yusra's unique genetic makeup provided her with a cloaking ability that would ultimately allow her to go invisible at will.

The young Sulaiman was a human ball of excitement. His determination was unrivaled, and he was the spitting image of the grandfather whose name he bore. In addition to strength of will, Sulaiman inherited a number of his grandfather's redeeming qualities: faith, patience, compassion and a host of others that endeared him to the vast majority of those with whom he would come in contact. However, the most important inheritance of all was the one that solidified the eternal link between the twins. Sulaiman inherited from his mother the exact heart that she inherited from her father. Thus, the twins were blessed with identical hearts.

Suley—as Yusra referred to him—would normally take the lead, even though Yusra was bigger in the beginning. He was naturally more curious and daring, not to mention the fact that they often played with physical objects, which Yusra hadn't learned to handle yet. Their connection was astounding. Each twin was pivotal in helping the other hone extraordinary skills in preparing for the destiny that lay ahead. Suley could see Yusra as easily as if she were flesh and bone—not realizing that almost no one else could. He patiently coached, as she tried again and again to handle new toys he wanted them to play with. Eventually they figured out that practicing with feathers helped her gain dexterity more quickly.

His unique bond with Yusra sharpened Suley's senses as well as his reflexes. There wasn't a single child his age with comparable dexterity, agility, intuition, or coordination anywhere. Bilal doted on him, enamored with his son's ability to match prowess with boys twice his age or older. In every way, the twins brought out the best in one another, and they were inseparable.

Samaa was ecstatic to have the home vibrant with life again; and even more so when she learned that Bilal and Nejimah were permanently moving in. The move felt right for everyone—especially the twins.

One night, there was a tap at Samaa's window. It was Hakeem. This was an unusual hour for a visit, so she knew it was important. Before going out, she checked on Yusra to make sure she didn't come back to the room and find her mother missing. Yusra was fine. She and Suley were snuggled beside Nejimah, who was reading their favorite bedtime stories to them. This would keep them occupied for at least thirty minutes. So Samaa returned to the room, floated through the window and onto the slanted rooftop, where Hakeem sat waiting.

She immediately noticed the look of concern on his face and asked what was wrong. He delayed for a second, blowing a puff of pixie dust at a firefly passing in front of him. Then, in a somber tone that could only accompany bad news, he revealed, "I'm hearing that Kibr is back, and apparently he's been asking about the twins."

"Kibr? I thought he was dead."

"Obviously not."

"Well, what does he want with the twins—and how does he know anything about them?"

"Samaa, everyone knows about them. They're always together. She goes to school with him, to the masjid … everywhere. There isn't a single jinni who doesn't know about them—and even some humans are suspicious."

"Maybe a little, but Nejimah's good about deflecting suspicion. In public, Yusra is an imaginary friend. That's it."

"Yes. Nejimah does an excellent job, but that's not what we're talking about. People aren't stupid, Samaa. They can see the boy is special, and they know it's more than that."

"But what does he want with them? They're babies!"

"They're not babies. They're children, growing faster everyday. More importantly, they're Sulaiman's children. What are you not understanding here? There's evil in the world—among men and among jinn. They hated your marriage, they hated your husband, and they hate your children. These creatures are vile. They're filled with racist jealousy, and the twins epitomize everything they despise.

199

Listen to me. If we can't protect them, Suley and Yusra are in grave danger."

No one knew the exact story of Kibr, except that he disappeared after Sulaiman died. It was widely assumed that the angel of death (Malakul Maut) had taken his soul along with Sulaiman's that day. If that wasn't the case, there was definitely a need for concern.

Kibr was pure evil, manifest in the form of the most wretched arrogance. Only the most heinous jinn could stand being in his presence, and they looked up to him. They lavished him with praise—almost as much as he showered upon himself. Nothing vexed him more than being defeated by Sulaiman's unwavering faith. Sulaiman was a glaring stain on Kibr's record, and though he pretended otherwise, he was embarrassed by it. His hatred for the man he once shadowed permeated his core.

He told elaborate stories, bragging to his entourage about the harm he inflicted upon Sulaiman. Many presumed the stories to be rife with embellishment. However, the infamous destruction of Sulaiman's marriage was a story corroborated by Umm Lahab. Kibr loved recounting it, and he laughed hysterically whenever he did. Apparently, Sulaiman was steeped in heartache to the extent he couldn't walk. Kibr claimed that the man crawled on the floor for days. So he lassoed the "filthy mud creature" and rode him around the house like an animal. This vicious demon would do anything to tarnish the name of Sulaiman Sanders.

In the weeks that followed, the family remained on high alert with all things concerning the twins. Yusra was no longer allowed to attend Suley's classes. In fact, she wasn't allowed outside the home without Samaa. The children didn't like it, but their parents insisted that the new rules were necessary to keep everyone safe. One afternoon, Yusra sat staring out the window, longing for Suley to return from school and asked, "Mommy, why don't you like for me to learn the Qur'an anymore?"

"Baby, I love for you to learn the Qur'an."

"But you said I can't go."

"Come here, baby. Sit with me and let me hold you. Do you remember the time when the dog came out from the neighbor's yard?"

"Mommy, it was terrible! We were so scared, and that dog could see me, Mommy. He chased me and Suley and he was mean."

"I know, baby. Well right now Mommy's a little scared, because there's another dog and he wants to chase us. So we have to be very careful. OK? You're gonna go back to school with Suley soon, but I need you to be patient, sweetheart. We have to wait a little longer to make sure the dog isn't coming."

There were only two weeks left before Ramadan, and it was a race against time, as Kibr was desperate to make something happen before the Islamic holy month. Unfortunately for him, he was no longer permitted to enter Sulaiman's home. A protective barrier prevented him from setting foot anywhere on the premises. So he hid out of sight in a yard nearby—plotting his next move. Day after day, he spied on the twins, memorizing their schedules and timing their every move. He hated them intensely—their smiling faces and the familiar hearts beating inside them. Finally, his plan was complete—a fool-proof conspiracy—with only one day left before Ramadan.

Bilal sat down in the vestibule of the masjid, putting on his shoes after Dhuhr prayer. Afterwards, he strolled across the campus to the primary school to pick up Suley. As usual, Suley was roughhousing with Firas—playing tug of war with a rubber dinosaur they both claimed to have first. Firas was the tallest kid in kindergarten and Suley was the youngest, at only four years old. Suley maneuvered around a bean bag, causing Firas to lose his footing, and wrested the toy free. Then he ran to the teacher yelling, "Khala Aisha, I had it first."

At that very moment, Suley looked up and saw Bilal walking through the classroom door. "Daddy!" he screamed with excitement, as he dropped the dinosaur and raced to see his father. He jumped into his dad's open arms, giving him a big hug. Bilal collected Suley's belongings and checked in with the teacher. "Sulaiman is very bright, very intelligent" she expressed. "I'm noticing that if he isn't challenged, he gets bored quickly. This young man is perhaps the most energetic child I have ever taught—seriously. I keep looking for the battery in him so I can turn it off," she laughed. Then, she walked around her desk and grabbed a blue ball, the approximate size of a grapefruit. "Brother Bilal, Sulaiman is not allowed to bring this back to school. It was too much of a distraction today. Otherwise, he had a pretty good day." She handed the ball to Suley, who reached for it with one hand while the other clung to his father's neck.

Kibr had been waiting outside the Islamic school for hours, and once Bilal exited the building, Kibr sped off en route to The Meadows. His minions had taken their places and were ready to execute the plan.

As the car pulled around the corner onto Sprite Meadow, Yusra's eyes lit up. She was always happy to see Suley coming home from school. Because of the new rules, she could no longer go. So she walked with him to the car every morning and waited in the driveway every afternoon.

Meanwhile, on a neighboring street, a young man strapped on his helmet and kicked his leg over the seat of his motorcycle. The qareen hanging from the back of his jacket was responsible for enticing him with drugs. Unfortunately, he listened to the whispers, allowing himself to be deceived. Heavily under the influence of hallucinogens, he turned the key and pressed the start button. No sooner did the bike start rolling, than the jinni jumped inside the helmet and took advantage of the young man's compromised mental state. With the qareen now in control of the motorcycle, it quickly approached maximum acceleration. As it rounded the first corner, Kibr burst from a tree and perched himself on the front of the motorcycle fairing.

Bilal pulled into the driveway and got out of the car to retrieve the bags from the back seat. Noticing the gorgeous red sunset behind him, he stopped for a second to admire it. Yusra rushed to the passenger door to meet Suley getting out of the car. She was so excited she accidentally knocked his ball from his hands and into the driveway. At the same time, the motorcycle came roaring around the second corner and onto Sprite Meadow Court. The ball bounced and rolled down the driveway and into the street. The twins darted down the driveway chasing after it. Watching the scene unfold before her eyes, Nejimah gasped, as her heart skipped a beat. "Sulaiman, no!" she screamed as she rushed into the street after the twins.

The desperation in Nejimah's tone alerted Samaa, who looked up from where she normally sat to wait with Yusra. The motorcycle ripped down the street at full throttle, heading directly for the twins. Kibr was perched on the front, holding a jinn dagger. Samaa channelled her energy into an instantaneous burst and hurled herself in the direction of the motorcycle. She shot into the street like a rocket. Kibr smiled. For years, he had wished to destroy her, and she was nanoseconds away from his claws. He flicked his wrist and stabbed into the air, realizing too late that she wasn't aiming for him. Samaa burst into the helmet, jarring the qareen loose, and the motorcyclist regained control of his own mind.

As the bike swerved away from the twins, Nejimah clutched her son frantically, fearing the tragedy that might have been. Yusra jumped into her arms as well, sensing her sister's fear. Holding both of the children, Nejimah turned to join her husband, who approached from the driveway. As the motorcycle swerved, Kibr jumped from the fairing and burst into the air, in a last-ditch effort. There was no way he would allow this opportunity to slip through his fingers. He fired through the air like a bullet, with his jinn dagger clinched in his hand, intent on piercing the heart of Yusra.

As he sat in his mother's arms, looking over her shoulder, Suley could see the evil demon approaching. He screamed and buried his face her garment. At the same time, Samaa stood up on the corner—where the momentum had thrown her from the helmet. She turned to look for Yusra and froze at the sight of Kibr approaching her daughter. She cried out to Allah with everything inside her, beseeching the Creator for help. In that very instant, Kibr's wrists and ankles were locked in chains as he was dragged away. The sun had set, marking the beginning of Ramadan. For the next thirty days, no one would need to worry about Kibr—or any of the evil jinn.

CHAPTER NINETEEN

amaa stood in awe, looking at her daughter held safely in Nejimah's arms. The motorist collected himself, after almost hitting a tree, and sped away. Suley was held, cradled in his mother's embrace, with his arms clinched around her neck. Yusra mimicked Suley, as she had never seen him so afraid. Fortunately for her, she missed the visual of Kibr's violent attempt on her life. Suley was less fortunate. He saw the treachery in Kibr's eyes as he was chained and dragged away.

Samaa stared at Nejimah. Nejimah stared back, with a sense that something was awry. She suspected jinn were involved in the motorcycle incident, but had no idea how close her little sister had come to losing her life. Samaa couldn't move. She stood frozen on the corner—stunned and in shock.

Nejimah sent the twins inside and proceeded walking to the corner. But as soon as she started down the driveway, she saw Samaa collapse to the ground. Instinctively, she started to run, but all of a sudden, she stopped. Reality set in. Samaa was invisible. So how exactly was Nejimah planning to help? Actually, she couldn't. There was nothing she could do.

Her father's widow lay lifeless on the ground a few paces away. Nejimah continued approaching slowly and silently began to pray. Then, incredibly, Samaa's being lifted from the concrete. She was still unconscious. Her arms and legs dangled as she floated through the air. Nejimah looked on, bewildered; as the lifeless jinni floated past her and up to the door of their home. It almost appeared as if she were being carried.

Rushing to the front door, Nejimah ran inside to get Suley. She discreetly enlisted his help—preventing Yusra from seeing her mother this way. "Do you see anything, Suley?" she asked.

"Yes Ma'am, it's Uncle. He wants to come inside." It was Hakeem requesting permission to take Samaa to her room. He had raced to The Meadows after word of Kibr spread throughout the community. He arrived fearing the worst when his saw his niece unconscious, but Alhamdulillah, she had only fainted. Nejimah opened the door, welcoming Hakeem into their home. He glided up the stairwell, carrying Samaa into her room, where she quickly regained consciousness.

The next morning, the family awakened to the first day of fasting. It was the blessed month of Ramadan, which ushered in magnificent bounties from the favors of Allah, the Most Merciful. In Ramadan, everything felt different. Although only one day removed from the horrible event, their hearts completely forgot about Kibr. It was as if his evil never existed. Ramadan has that effect: replacing evil and unhappiness with tranquility. A sense of love and togetherness covered them all, and for an entire month, happiness followed this family wherever they went.

As is usually the case, the sacred days of Ramadan passed quickly. Samaa sat in the window, peering out at a mother blue jay teaching her fledgling to fly. It was a beautiful dance of love and trust—a poignant reminder on this final day of the Islamic holy month. Yusra came over and sat in her mother's lap. She fidgeted with her favorite feather that Suley had found by the creek. Samaa stroked the cheeks of her precious little one and kissed her on the forehead. Tomorrow would be Eid and she was having mixed feelings. The final day of Ramadan is always a tradeoff: the excitement of Eid for the sadness of bidding the blessed month farewell. This year, however, presented an additional conundrum: Kibr.

There was no question that the diabolical jinni would return, but the family remained resolute. They would not allow the threat of evil to relegate their manner of worship or dampen the joy of celebration. If they had chosen the side of the Almighty, what threat exists more powerful than He? There is no defeat in the company of the faithful—only trials. Besides, they were prepared. They enlisted friends and family to help guard against potential danger, and the twins had practiced safety drills the entire month.

The weather was incredible, as another joyous Eid Day wound into nightfall. The crisp, cool breeze, shuffling through the trees, was a breath of fresh air. Samaa smiled at Hakeem as Yusra skipped along the molecules, holding her mother's hand. This day was everything Samaa had hoped for; she was entirely fulfilled. The joy she felt inside was matched only by feelings of love and pure gratitude. After all, there was so much to be thankful for. She could still hear the laughter of all the happy children playing with one another, especially her Yusra. They were finally making their way back home after a long day of celebrating.

As they arrived at the house, Bilal's car rounded the corner and gradually came to a stop in the driveway. Suley was in the back seat waving—excited to show Yusra all the presents he received. The two mothers locked eyes and breathed a collective sigh of relief, as each had been worried about the other. Nejimah exited the vehicle. Samaa kissed her on the cheek while the twins happily recapped their adventures. The mothers also shared a moment of comradery while Bilal unloaded the car. Then, just as they were about to go inside, Samaa looked up. What she saw left her stunned, in momentary paralysis. Hakeem saw it too.

An angel descended from the clouds and into the front yard. Not just any angel ... Malakul Maut. A million thoughts raced through her mind as Samaa cautioned the family to be still. She waited to see what he would do, but the angel of death did nothing. He leaned against the corner of the garage and waited.

It occurred to Samaa that Kibr might be hiding, waiting for an opportunity to strike. She grabbed the twins and reminded them of the game they practiced in Ramadan. They were prepared for this moment. Every member of the family began to lift their voice and say, "*Aoothu Billahi minash-shaitanir rajeem.*" This is the defense against the satans. The twins made it a competition, seeing who could say it the loudest. Bilal joined in. Hakeem joined in. Everyone rebuked the demonic evil, in calling for the protection of Allah. After awhile, Kibr couldn't bear it. "Shut up!" he roared, as he emerged from the trunk of the tree that disguised him.

Immediately, Samaa sent the twins inside, cautioning Nejimah to keep them safe. Under no circumstances should either of them be allowed outside. Hakeem approached Kibr, attempting to restrain him, but the elder was no match for the arrogant one. Kibr easily freed himself and bashed Hakeem's head with a mighty blow—leaving him unconscious. Samaa turned, looking at Malakul Maut to see what he would do. So far, nothing. Alhamdulillah, her uncle was still alive. Then she shifted her attention to Kibr.

The evil jinni approached Samaa, howling with laughter, as if mocking her. She was unfazed and unafraid— laser focused. There was no way he was getting anywhere near the twins as long as she was alive. The energy channelled into her core, as she fueled a burst to defend her family. Kibr continued his approach. Samaa fired, propelling herself so fast that he barely saw it coming. She whacked him in the side of his head and knocked him back a few feet. It didn't hurt, but he was surprised—he realized he had underestimated her strength. Kibr wiped the silly smirk off his face and made a beeline for the house. He was done with the child's play.

A renewed sense of urgency boiled inside, as Samaa swelled with the largest energy burst she'd ever channelled. She shot like a meteor with a tail of fire and crashed into his back, tumbling him to the ground. Now THAT hurt. Kibr was shaken and dizzy. He was furious as he gathered his bearings. He was now hell-bent on putting Samaa in her place. That was exactly what she was aiming for. She wanted him focused on her and not the twins.

He levitated high off the ground, fueling an enormous energy burst and daring her to come closer. The clever female ignored his threats and played to her own strengths. She stayed on the ground, fueling a burst of her own, as she waited for his next move. He fired, blazing through the air. She fired out of the way. He fired again—faster this time. Same result. He became more agitated with every near-miss. Samaa was the fastest jinni he had ever encountered.

Raging with ferocity, Kibr was done playing this game. He lowered himself in the street, facing the house, swelling with energy. Samaa scrambled, taking a defensive position by the garage. She carefully timed his movements, and when he fired, she fired directly into his path. They ricocheted off one another like pinballs, leaving Samaa badly hurt. She was in excruciating pain but quickly regrouped. He could see that she was hurting, and her bursts were getting weaker. Kibr, on the other hand, was barely getting started.

The maleficent energy inside him accumulated into an enormous burst—one that would likely put an end to any jinni in its path. It was almost overwhelming to behold, as Samaa braced and readied herself. She turned to the side—glancing at Malakul Maut. Then she looked into the sky and prayed:

"Oh Allah, forgive me for my sins. Grant me a life … and a death with which you are well pleased. Protect the babies inside this house, Lord, and never leave them vulnerable to those who would harm them. I bear witness, there is no god except Allah, and that Muhammad is His messenger and servant."

Kibr fired. Samaa fired. They met in a cataclysmic explosion that crossed between dimensions—suspending them in a realm between the seen and unseen. Hakeem regained consciousness. He looked above the driveway, at the extraordinary burst of energy encapsulating the two at war with one another. The commotion outside was nerve-racking and Nejimah couldn't stand it anymore. She left the twins in Bilal's care and ran outside to investigate.

Suddenly, in a moment eerily similar to a previous event, the bladed wing of an angel came piercing through the sky, like a thunderbolt. It sliced into the heart of the explosion; and Samaa was knocked loose. She came flying out of the barrier and slammed into the grass. She was barely conscious but struggled to gather her bearings and locate Kibr. When she finally laid eyes on him, the razor-sharp wing was pulling out from his corpse and Malakul Maut was taking his soul. "Allahu Akbar," she sighed in exhaustion, "Allahu Akbar."

As Samaa lay in the grass, breathing a sigh of relief, every inch of her being was in pain. Her head was pounding and her core felt like it was placed in a grinder. Her fingers and toes tingled. Even her eyes seemed to be in pain. Everything hurt. She tried lying as still as possible because the slightest movement intensified her suffering. Still, she was grateful. Kibr was gone forever, and her precious Yusra was safe inside. For Samaa, that was worth the world and everything in it. Besides, wounds heal and the pain eventually goes away. She closed her eyes and tried to relax.

Moments later, a warm sensation covered her hand. The gentle touch of love had come to the rescue. Samaa opened her eyes to find Nejimah's smiling face staring back at her. How beautiful it was to see the love and admiration in her eyes ... the daughter of Sulaiman. Nejimah held Samaa's hand as they allowed their silence to communicate emotions too magnificent for words.

From the corner of her eye, Samaa caught a glimpse of something moving. Delicately, she turned her head and noticed Hakeem. She'd forgotten that he had escorted her home from the Eid celebration. Alhamdulillah, he was safe, but he had a strange expression on his face. He seemed worried. She continued scanning the periphery and noticed Malakul Maut. He was standing near the garage, where he'd been all night; but that was peculiar, because she'd watched him collect Kibr's soul already. It took her a minute to put it all together, but ultimately, Samaa realized that her own soul would not survive the night. Kibr's jinn dagger was protruding from a wound in her core—a wound that was most assuredly fatal.

Samaa squeezed Nejimah's hand, pulling it next to her cheek, and then flush against her ear. Nejimah understood she was listening for her pulse. So she cradled Samaa, helping reposition her head, and pinning Samaa's ear against her chest. There it was … the indelible sound of the dreamer's heart. Samaa closed her eyes and listened, reminiscing of her husband and the endless love they shared.

Nejimah was in awe of this moment and all that it entailed. She marveled at the flash of light that spewed Samaa from it, altering her appearance. Now visible to the ordinary eye, Samaa glistened like a firefly. She was covered in a radiant glow, more beautiful than a sunset—almost angelic. In a moment when words seemed futile, Nejimah ventured to share a few. "Daddy would be so proud of you. I wish he could see you now … Insha-Allah soon. Samaa, what do you say to someone who has just saved your life and everything you love? I don't know the answer to that, but I know that I love you, and my life is richer for having known you. You are so beautiful; Allah has honored you tonight."

Samaa opened her eyes and looked at Nejimah with a partial smile on her face. Then she began to deliver her last wishes: "Nejimah, you're her mother now. Take care of her for me. Be everything that I would be and more. Be diligent … be vigilant … and don't feel sorry for her. If anyone knows the pain of losing a mother, it's you, her sister. So empathize with her, but don't be a pushover. Your sister is capable of greatness. Require that of her, as with Suley. I need you to be a mother to your little sister. Guide her. Allow her to see her father through you. Allow her to see herself in you. Allah has placed an incredible responsibility in your hands, and you will be a phenomenal mother to both of them. For all that you are and all you will become, I love you. Come on, pick me up … let's go and talk to them."

Samaa disguised her injury as Nejimah helped her into the house. Bilal met them in the foyer, and for the first time, he saw Samaa. "Bilal, this is my stepmother, Samaa," Nejimah introduced. Bilal greeted her as they continued into the living room, where Nejimah helped Samaa onto the sofa.

Noticing Samaa's discomfort, the twins asked what was wrong. Nejimah redirected, instructing them to gather around for a family discussion. As they came together, Samaa could see that Malakul Maut had come inside and was standing in the foyer. She would need to make her message brief: "Yusra, you are Mommy's joy, and Suley, you are my hero. Always remember how much I love you. I want you both to know how very special you are. Yusra, you can do things that Suley can't, and Suley, you can do things that Yusra can't; that is why Allah has made you close. When you work together, there's nothing you won't accomplish. Do you understand?"

They nodded in agreement. Then Samaa turned to Yusra. Gazing in her daughter's eyes, she said, "Listen to me, sweetie. Listen to your mommy carefully, OK? Never EVER be ashamed of who you are. Allah created you on purpose … and with purpose. There is no one in the world exactly like you, and that makes you special. Don't let anyone make you feel like you don't belong; be proud of what makes you different. Be grateful to Allah for your uniqueness. Suley, you have to look after Yusra. Make sure she remembers that Allah chose her to be special, and defend her, like the hero you are. Defend her against the humans and the jinn. And Yusra, you have to look after Suley. Remind him of the same and defend him against the same. OK?"

Again, they nodded in the affirmative. Samaa continued: "Allah has created every one of us and made us a part of this incredible family. Do you know what that means? It means we have a responsibility. When Allah gives you something special, he couples it with a special job that allows you to use it. I have seen your heart, Suley … and your heart, Yusra … and your heart, Nejimah. And I have seen the heart of Sulaiman, the dreamer. They are all the same heart. That is a gift from Allah. DO NOT let that gift go to waste. Clean your hearts with kindness and with love and forgiveness, and by helping others. Will you do that?"

They all agreed. Then Samaa made a typical request. "So tell me something good," she prompted. "What is it that I always tell you?"

Suley spoke first: "Always pray to Allah for what you want, because Allah wants to give you what you want?"

"Yes, very good. And what else?"

Yusra volunteered next: "Always do good, even when it's hard, and Allah will make it easier if you practice doing good."

"That's also very good, but there's one more. Let me give you a hint: what do we say when others tell us something is impossible?"

The entire household replied, "Anything is possible by the permission of Allah."

"Yes—that's it. That is the message of our family to this world. Anything—*absolutely anything*—is possible, by the permission of Allah!"

These were her last words, and with that, Samaa was gone.

DISCUSSION QUESTIONS

Book Club Discussion

1. Who is your favorite character and why? Second favorite?

2. What is the most memorable scene in the book and what emotions did you feel when you read it? Did you stop reading and reflect or continue to see what happened next?

3. What did you like most about the story? What did you like least?

4. Why do you think the author wrote this story and what (if anything) does it say about him?

5. Have any of your perceptions changed after reading this story? Please elaborate.

6. Have you ever had dreams with vivid details that you could remember after waking? What about deja vu?

Classroom Discussion

7. One of the most pronounced symbols of redemption in the book occurs when Umm Lahab changes her name to Nurah and dedicates her life to wearing hijab—even though hijab is not a requirement for her. Discuss her state of mind in making these decisions and what are some of the other symbols of redemption in this story?

8. Celine, Shifaa, Nejimah, Samaa and Nurah are all individuals whose lives were directly or indirectly impacted by Sulaiman prior to their embracing Islam. Discuss Sulaiman's role in connecting them with Islam. Also, elaborate on the various ways a Muslim might inspire someone else to see Islam in a more positive light.

9. The pain of a broken heart can be catastrophic in a person's life. How might that affect one's faith? What about their behavior? Give an example from the story and describe how you might have handled having your heart broken in a similar fashion.

10. What is Sulaiman's best quality? What about Hakeem, Shifaa, Samaa, etc? What are their character flaws or areas where they need to improve? Which character did you identify with the most?

11. What was the most important message in this story or what message resonated with you most? Is that

something you feel can be actionable in your life moving forward?

12. There are occasions when Samaa reflects on the challenges of an interracial marriage. She also states a very powerful message to Yusra about being proud of how Allah has created her. Discuss the harm that racism causes in the community and how to combat people who behave like Kibr and his minions.

13. What other questions can you come up with to continue the discussion?

AUTHOR'S NOTE

Dear Reader,

I'm filled with emotion as I sit here staring out of my window, reflecting on our journey together. Curiosity fuels my imagination as I wonder what you might be feeling after witnessing the last few moments of Samaa's life. Are you missing her already, or have you found comfort in the knowledge that she will soon be joining her beloved Sulaiman—to be with him forever?

Writing my first novel has been a whirlwind adventure into my own heart—into the caverns of my memory that hold secrets I thought I'd forgotten. Believe it or not, I was never going to write this story. Until now, I was never a lover of fiction. Traditionally, it's been my view that "real life" is far more interesting than the things people "make up." Then one day, I sat at my desktop and allowed the story inside of me to tell itself. Two weeks later, almost twenty five thousand words had poured out of me. And that was just the beginning. I'm hooked.

If the characters in my story have taught you anything about me, then you know (of a certainty) that I don't believe in coincidence. This moment between us is destiny…nothing less. Thank you for climbing aboard and skipping along the molecules with me. I appreciate the gift of your time and your willingness to share my world more than you'll ever know.

The best part is that the story doesn't end here. I'm on the edge of my seat with excitement—can't wait to share what the future holds for Suley and Yusra. Be on the lookout for the second episode in the *Unhaunted Series,* and please reach out to let me know how you felt about book one. There's so much more that I'd like to share. So let's keep in touch. Find me at:

peacepearlsusa@gmail.com
Instagram: @ibrahimultifaceted